PRAISE FOR USA TODAY AND WALL STREET JOURNAL BESTSELLING AUTHOR JAN MORAN

Seabreeze Inn and *Coral Cottage* series

"A wonderful story… Will make you feel like the sea breeze is streaming through your hair." – Laura Bradbury, Bestselling Author

"A novel that gives fans of romantic sagas a compelling voice to follow." – *Booklist*

"An entertaining beach read with multi-generational context and humor." – *InD'Tale* Magazine

"Wonderful characters and a sweet story." – Kellie Coates Gilbert, Bestselling Author

"A fun read that grabs you at the start." – Tina Sloan, Author and Award-Winning Actress

"Jan Moran is the queen of the epic romance." —Rebecca Forster, *USA Today* Bestselling Author

"The women are intelligent and strong. At the core is a strong, close-knit family." — Betty's Reviews

The Chocolatier

"A delicious novel, makes you long for chocolate." – *Ciao Tutti*

"Smoothly written…full of intrigue, love, secrets, and romance." – *Lekker Lezen*

The Winemakers

"Readers will devour this page-turner as the mystery and passions spin out." – *Library Journal*

"As she did in *Scent of Triumph*, Moran weaves knowledge of wine and winemaking into this intense family drama." – *Booklist*

The Perfumer: Scent of Triumph

"Heartbreaking, evocative, and inspiring, this book is a powerful journey." – Allison Pataki, *NYT* Bestselling Author of *The Accidental Empress*

"A sweeping saga of one woman's journey through World War II and her unwillingness to give up even when faced with the toughest challenges." — Anita Abriel, Author of *The Light After the War*

"A captivating tale of love, determination and reinvention." — Karen Marin, Givenchy Paris

"A stylish, compelling story of a family. What sets this apart is the backdrop of perfumery that suffuses the story with the delicious aromas – a remarkable feat!" — Liz Trenow, *NYT* Bestselling Author of *The Forgotten Seamstress*

"Courageous heroine, star-crossed lovers, splendid sense of time and place capturing the unease and turmoil of the 1940s; HEA." — *Heroes and Heartbreakers*

BOOKS BY JAN MORAN

20th-Century Historical

Hepburn's Necklace

The Chocolatier

The Winemakers: A Novel of Wine and Secrets

The Perfumer: Scent of Triumph

USA TODAY BESTSELLING AUTHOR

JAN MORAN

Coral WEDDINGS

THE CORAL COTTAGE AT SUMMER BEACH
BOOK FOUR

CORAL WEDDINGS

CORAL COTTAGE AT SUMMER BEACH, BOOK 4

JAN MORAN

Library of Congress Cataloging-in-Publication Data
Moran, Jan.
/ by Jan Moran

ISBN 978-1-64778-061-6 (ebook)
ISBN 978-1-64778-062-3 (paperback)
ISBN 978-1-64778-063-0 (hardcover)
ISBN 978-1-64778-064-7 (large print)
ISBN 978-1-64778-065-4 (audiobook)

Published by Sunny Palms Press. Cover design by Sleepy Fox Studios. Cover
images copyright Deposit Photos.

Sunny Palms Press
9663 Santa Monica Blvd STE 1158
Beverly Hills, CA 90210 USA
www.sunnypalmspress.com
www.JanMoran.com

1

*F*rom her kitchen in the Coral Cafe, Marina looked outside to see a yellow food truck emblazoned with a logo of a submarine sandwich and the words, *Yellow Submarines*, pull into the parking area. With a surge of excitement, she quickly finished a tray of canapés for a friend's wedding and set it aside. After shrugging out of her stained chef jacket, she hurried toward the vehicle.

A trim woman stepped out to greet her. She wore jeans and a bright shirt that matched her vehicle.

Marina shielded her eyes against the summer sun reflecting off the ocean beyond. "Thanks for bringing the truck by for me to see."

The woman introduced herself as Judith. Her dark blue eyes were a startling contrast with her dark, silver-shot hair, and she had a happy air about her. "No problem. I was on my way to a catering event I'm doing tonight. It's my last one." Judith opened the rear door. "Have a look inside."

Marina stepped up into the mobile kitchen, trying to imagine what it would be like to expand her Coral Cafe onto wheels. Having had some success with her cafe, she was eager to build on that, although a food truck would be a financial gamble.

Still, with the seasonality of Summer Beach and her cafe, the risk was one she needed to take to secure her future. A food truck could go anywhere. If it rained for a week at the beach on her outdoor cafe, she wouldn't lose a quarter of her month's earnings. She could drive inland to sunnier skies.

As Marina inspected the workspace and appliances, Judith pointed out various features that checked a lot of boxes on Marina's shopping list. Inside, the vehicle had a wide service window, good ventilation, and stainless-steel counters. Growing more excited, she checked out the grill, deep fryer, refrigerator, freezer, and sink.

Marina was impressed, though she tried not to let her eagerness show. After some of the older used trucks she'd seen, this one seemed almost too good to be true. Was it?

"This truck looks immaculate. You seem to have taken excellent care of it."

Judith acknowledged the compliment with a smile. "That's because Bessie—that's what I call her—has taken good care of me. I bought her right after my divorce. I hadn't worked in years, and no one was eager to hire a fifty-year-old. The only thing I knew how to do was make sandwiches."

Marina wasn't too far behind her, though she'd had a career as a news anchor in San Francisco. Still, after she'd lost her job not long ago, she'd had few offers at her age, especially after her embarrassing on-air meltdown. But that was in the past.

She ran her hand along a pizza oven where she could make her popular seafood pizzas. This food truck could be part of the bright future she planned. "So why are you selling it?"

"I'm moving."

"And you can't take it with you?"

"Not to New Zealand." Judith grinned. "This has been a

great gig, but I'm getting married. Hope springs eternal, right? He's a chef from New Zealand, and we're buying a restaurant in Queenstown, so Bessie stays here. I never dreamed of marrying again, but then, I never thought I'd be divorced. Life has thrown a lot of surprises at me. Still, I'm happy how things turned out."

"That I can understand." Marina's life had also changed dramatically.

She disembarked and circled the food truck. Outside, the truck had solar panels on the roof and a canopy that extended over the service window. She tried to imagine the vehicle with her vivid coral color scheme.

Judith followed her out and ran a hand over the still shiny paint. "I went through a lot with this truck. In fact, this led me to my new husband."

"How did that happen?"

A fond look filled Judith's face. "I'd pulled up to a baseball game where his grandson was playing. Harold ordered a meatball sub with extra sauce. Said it was the best one he'd ever had. I told him the meatballs were my grandmother's recipe. Soon we were trading recipes and techniques, and a few months later, we were planning our wedding. When I was married, I spent my time caring for my husband's parents and mine before they passed. So now I get a second chance with a great guy and his kids. I really love them all." She patted a fender. "Bessie is good luck."

"I'll keep that in mind." Marina smiled. "I can always do with a bit of luck."

"I've had several couples look at it." After a brief pause, Judith asked, "Are you married?"

"Widowed," came Marina's automatic reply of more than two decades. "But I'm seeing someone pretty special now." Her heart quickened even as she thought of Jack.

A smile spread across Judith's face. "I hope it works out for you, too. Would you be operating this truck together?"

Marina chuckled. "He's not good with food. But he has an appetite that makes up for it. I enjoy cooking for people." She tried out all her new dishes on Jack and his son Leo, who had a surprisingly good palette for an eleven-year-old. "To me, well-prepared food is one of the languages of love."

"It sure has been for me," Judith agreed.

Marina did a cursory inspection of the body and systems, wondering what Jack would think of this. They'd fallen into an easy routine the last few months. Though he often spoke of their future together, he hadn't made any firm commitments. But then, neither had she.

Recently, her grandmother questioned if Jack might be taking her for granted. While Marina didn't think so, the idea stuck in her mind. She loved Jack, but she might have been too available and accommodating. However, Marina wasn't one to wait for a man to make a decision. She'd always had to provide for herself and her twins.

This was her new chapter of life, and she was determined to forge ahead and expand her Coral Cafe footprint and brand.

"What do you think?" Judith asked.

"It's nice, but I'll need to have it inspected. And I'd have to paint or wrap it to match the branding for my existing cafe." Marina's head ached at the thought of another large expense. "Are you negotiable on the price?"

"I could knock some off for that."

"That would help." Marina had penciled out her financial projections, and the bank had approved a loan, which she thought she could pay off fairly quickly. She'd done her research, yet this was still a big step for her.

Her existing cafe was close to the beach and tourists, so she was thinking about other venues, including the Seashell amphitheater that her sister Kai and her fiancé Axe were operating. She was already providing premade boxed dinners, so she knew there was an opportunity to build on that. Her mind was full of other options.

"How was your sandwich business?" Marina asked.

"Pretty good. I did the usual lunches near office buildings, but the real money is in special events. Parties, weddings, bar mitzvahs."

Those were also on Marina's list, along with other ideas. "Did you serve at many weddings?"

"Surprisingly, yes. A lot of people want to provide food for guests. A food truck is a fun option, especially for small, casual affairs like beach weddings. They often want more upscale food, though. Probably more like what you serve."

That was true. Marina had talked to a wedding planner in Summer Beach who was interested in booking her. Having a kitchen on wheels would expand her opportunities, and now that she was training another cook, she could branch out.

Fortunately, the cafe was doing well during the summer season. She was determined to grow her off-season business now.

"I've had a couple of people look at the truck who haven't worked in food service before," Judith went on. "It might be against my interests, but I advised them to get a job in the industry first. I'd hate to sell this to someone who didn't know what to do with it. I had it outfitted just the way I wanted after getting some initial experience."

"It's obvious that a lot of thought went into it."

"What do you plan on serving out of the truck?"

"Mostly SoCal beach fare." Marina ticked off some of her popular menu items on her fingers. "Grilled kabobs, veggie burgers, and protein and fruit smoothies. Crab cakes and gourmet seafood pizza are a couple of my specialties. Chopped salads, cheese boards, and any sort of sliders are popular. I serve them with sweet potato fries and aioli."

Judith looked impressed. "That kind of menu would do

well at the beach and special venues. There are quite a few art shows and wine festivals you could work."

"Those are good ideas." With the mild weather in Southern California, there were many events year-round in nearby communities, just not as many in Summer Beach.

"I'm curious," Judith said, nodding to the tables on the outdoor patio. "Why not just stick with the cafe?"

Marina had thought a lot about that. "The idea of expanding without the cost of physical overhead appeals to me. I have twins, and I want to put some money back for them. And for my eventual retirement, although I hope that's a long way off."

The food truck could provide a new source of revenue, which would be welcome with her daughter Heather still in college.

Judith squinted against the sun, seeming to weigh a decision. "If I don't sell the food truck before I leave, I plan to list it with a business broker. But since you have a cafe and know what you're doing, I believe you'd be a good fit. If you're serious about it."

"I sure am, but I also have a budget." It was a little scary, but Marina had confidence in the homework she'd done.

Judith dragged a toe in the sand in thought. "If you want the truck, I can reduce the price by the commission I would have paid to a broker. That would give you a terrific deal. I want to see this truck go to a good home. It meant a lot to me."

"I can tell." Marina smiled at her with a measure of gratitude. "And that price reduction would help a lot."

Judith gazed at the food truck with a wistful expression. "Bessie gave me the freedom to run my own business. I'm going to miss her."

Marina felt that way about her cafe, too. "I can send photos to let you know how she's doing."

A smile bloomed on the woman's face. "Would you? I'd

like to know this truck is helping another woman. She was so good to me."

Judith named a price that Marina thought was more than fair. Although her stomach was fluttering with equal measures of excitement and trepidation, she decided to take the leap.

Marina put out her hand to shake on the deal. "I have someone who can inspect Bessie right away, and as long as she checks out, I'll take her."

"Have them call me." Judith clasped her hand. "You've got yourself a deal." After trading information, she drove away.

Even though Marina was nearly bursting with excitement, she hurried to her kitchen to finish packing food for the wedding this evening. She was also attending as Jack's guest, so she had to shower and dress. Tonight was a special night for him. His son's mother, Vanessa, was getting married.

Through an open window, she could hear her youngest sister Kai singing in the shower on the second floor of their grandmother's beach house. Once Kai's show tunes stopped, it would be Marina's turn in the shower. She smiled at the happy sound. Her sister was a professional with a lovely voice. Although Marina felt like singing for joy, no one would want to hear her attempts.

As she worked, she tried to rein in her excitement; the food truck still had to pass inspection.

Just then, her son Ethan pulled into the driveway. He drove an SUV that could carry all the golf gear he usually carted around. He was a lanky young man with dark, golden blond hair and gray-blue eyes.

Seated next to him was his twin sister, Heather, whose similar eyes were stunning. Her long hair was pulled into a ponytail.

They had agreed to work the wedding this evening, which would be held at the Seabreeze Inn on the beach. Marina's Mini-Cooper wasn't much help for catering.

"Perfect timing," Marina called out as she walked toward them. She could hardly wait to share her news about the food truck.

LATER THAT EVENING, Marina sat with Jack on the patio of the Seabreeze Inn, a beautiful old grand dame of a beach house. A soft, balmy breeze rustled the palm trees surrounding the patio where guests were gathered for the sunset wedding of Vanessa Rodriguez and Dr. Noah Hess.

All the guests were taking their seats now. Marina's grandmother, the incomparable Ginger Delavie, sat on the other side of her. They were chatting with Ivy Bay, the proprietor of the inn and an old summer friend of Marina's. They'd met as teenagers and reconnected when Marina returned to Summer Beach.

Ivy leaned forward. "I couldn't resist taking a peek at your appetizers in the kitchen. They look delicious, especially the crab cakes and grilled shrimp cocktail. I had to try your prosciutto on mini-flatbread. That was really tasty."

"Thank you," Marina said, genuinely appreciative. "And I love your dress. It looks fabulous on you." The halter-neck style was a full-skirted floral cotton dress cinched at the waist.

Ivy fluffed the skirt as she spoke. "It's one of my mother's vintage dresses that she brought back from her honeymoon in Paris. I've always loved it, and she let me alter it to fit me this summer."

Ginger nodded approvingly. "Carlotta has always had excellent taste. It looks like one of Christian Dior's designs."

"That's exactly right," Ivy exclaimed.

While Ginger and Ivy continued to talk, Marina looked around, enjoying the lovely scene. This was a beach-style wedding, and all the women wore lightweight summer frocks.

Ginger looked elegant in a peach-colored sheath dress that brought out the highlights in her still-ginger-hued hair, and a triple strand of pearls like Jackie Kennedy might have worn. They were a tenth-anniversary gift from Bertrand, Marina knew. For herself, she'd chosen a slate-blue dress splashed with creamy lilies.

On the other side of her, Jack wore a pressed, open-collar shirt with linen trousers like most other men here. He reached for her hand.

"I'm glad Vanessa found someone who genuinely loves her." His voice was edged with emotion. "After all she's been through, she deserves this."

Marina was deeply happy for Vanessa, too. Dr. Noah Hess was a world-renowned medical researcher in Switzerland and had been part of the medical team that treated her. They had fallen in love during the process. Few thought she would recover, but Dr. Noah had discovered a new therapy. Fortunately, Vanessa responded to the treatment and was now in remission. Forever, Marina hoped, because Leo needed his mother.

"Sometimes all it takes is meeting the right person." Marina squeezed his hand.

Jack raised his brow and nodded thoughtfully. "Is that how you felt about Stan?"

Marina had meant Jack, but she still answered. "We were very much in love, and he was also my best friend. I've always wished that Heather and Ethan could have known their father."

Stan had died in Afghanistan before the twins were born. Marina had been so busy caring for them and working that she'd hardly had time to think of anything else.

Marina glanced back to see if her children had joined them for the ceremony.

They had. Heather and Ethan were seated in the last row with friends. They'd managed the arrangement of appetizers well. They helped Marina with events when they had time, although Ethan was almost entirely focused on his golf.

Heather was on summer break from college, but her life would soon change after graduation.

Just then, the music soared, and Marina turned with the rest of the small crowd that was gathered.

Leo walked with his mother toward the pastor, beaming as Vanessa tucked her arm through the small crook in her son's arm. He had grown and was only a few inches shorter than his mother.

Next to her, Jack swallowed hard. "He looks so grown up."

"And Vanessa looks beautiful."

The bride wore a diaphanous silk dress in a soft shade of buttercream. Vanessa's hair had grown back, and she wore a sparkly band that swept her short dark hair from her face. Marina had never seen her look happier.

Jack and Vanessa had once been colleagues. During one dangerous assignment that neither of them thought they would live through, they'd sought comfort with each other as bullets whizzed overhead.

A lifetime ago, as Vanessa once put it. It had only been one night, and she'd never told Jack they'd had a child. She'd simply left the position, and though they kept in touch for a little while, she never mentioned it to him.

It wasn't until Vanessa had been diagnosed with a life-threatening illness that she contacted Jack to meet his son. Vanessa was pragmatic; if she didn't survive, Leo would need his father.

Jack had been shocked and dismayed that she'd never told him. Still, Vanessa had been adamant that she'd never wanted to marry him or anyone else. Her parents wouldn't have accepted Jack anyway.

Vanessa's parents were both gone now. Marina admired how Jack had immediately risen to the challenge. Even though he was still learning how to be a father, he loved Leo.

At one time, Marina was concerned that Vanessa might have been in love with Jack. Knowing Jack, he would have felt a duty to marry her for Leo's sake, but Vanessa wouldn't hear of it. She'd always had her own mind and stood firm against marriage.

Until she met Dr. Noah.

The slight, bespectacled man beamed at his radiant bride-to-be as she walked toward him. Leo passed his mother's hand to the man who would become his stepfather before taking his seat beside Jack.

"How'd I do, Dad?" Leo whispered.

"You did great. I'm awfully proud of you, young man." Jack put his arm around Leo and hugged him close.

Watching the two of them, Marina's heart swelled with love. She got along well with Leo but thought the boy might need time to adjust to his new stepfather. Dr. Noah was a kind, brilliant man, and Marina was happy for all of them.

The ceremony soon got underway. Vanessa and Dr. Noah exchanged vows, touching Marina with their sincerity. From the corner of her eye, she saw Jack sniff and wipe his eyes. He still cared for Vanessa as a cherished friend and the mother of his child. Marina was glad for all of them that the situation had worked out for the best.

Jack's hand was warm, and she threaded her fingers with his, enjoying their connection. She wondered if they would have their turn someday.

Lately, Jack had been acting differently. Occasionally, he'd refer to their future together, yet he was very casual about it.

Ginger glanced at her, then at Jack and Leo. Her grandmother noticed and analyzed everything around her. Marina valued her opinion, and she knew Ginger adored Jack. He was illustrating the children's books she'd written over the years. Still, Ginger had high standards.

Jack might have been a highly talented investigative journalist, but he'd also confessed that he'd never stayed in one place or with one woman very long. That is, until he moved to Summer Beach to look after Leo.

The pastor was speaking now, giving Vanessa and Dr. Noah the final pronouncement of the union. When Vanessa kissed her new husband, Leo began clapping. Everyone laughed and joined in as Leo raced from his chair to join his mother and Dr. Noah. The three joined hands to walk down the aisle, and Leo was beaming.

"That's my boy," Jack said, chuckling. "Stealing the spotlight again just as he did at the holiday show."

Marina laughed. Leo was so precious to her. In the last year's holiday production at the Seashell, he played the part of Tiny Tim and displayed a natural aptitude for acting. Her sister Kai had directed Leo in the show. Through that experience, Vanessa became good friends with Kai, too.

"I couldn't have directed that better myself," Kai said. "I think the photographer got the shot, too."

Jack grinned. "I'm sure Vanessa will appreciate that."

While everyone congratulated the happy couple, Marina excused herself to check on the food. She trusted Heather and Ethan, but she wanted to make sure everything ran smoothly for Vanessa, who was taking photos with Dr. Noah and Leo.

While the small crowd mingled during the cocktail hour, Marina made her way through family and friends toward the kitchen. Inside, she spoke to Ivy's sister, Shelly, and their niece, Poppy. The three women were making sure that everyone was happy and comfortable.

Marina saw other guests at the inn, including a long-term resident, Gilda, who lived there with her Chihuahua. Pixie was a known kleptomaniac. The two often came to the cafe for lunch, and just the other day, Pixie had made off with a woman's shoe when she'd kicked it off under the table while eating.

On her way to Ivy's kitchen, Marina stopped to chat with Gilda. The woman was carrying Pixie in a pink backpack that matched the streaks in her hair. "Going out?"

"We're taking a walk for inspiration. It's such a beautiful

evening, and Pixie hasn't been out today except for her therapy appointment."

Pixie yapped as if to chastise Gilda.

"Poor baby." Marina scratched Pixie behind the ears while she spoke to Gilda. "How is your writing going?"

"I'm finishing an article for *Dog Lovers Monthly*. The editor also wants to feature some heart-filled short stories. Fiction is a change from my usual articles, but it should be fun to try. Maybe I'll work Scout into one."

Scout was Jack's lovable young Labrador retriever whose enthusiasm for life was as outsized as his huge puppy paws. "Jack and Leo would love that. If you do, I'll let it be a surprise. I know you like to write here at the inn, but you're welcome to bring your laptop to the cafe anytime."

Gilda smiled. "The change of pace might help the muse. Thanks." She angled her head toward the parlor, where an attractive man sat reading a book. "Have you seen the new pediatrician?"

Marina followed her gaze. Tall, long legs, chiseled chin. She noticed other women swiping glances at him.

Gilda continued, "Bennett is helping him find a house. He's taking over Dr. Dede's practice when she retires. And he's single." She nudged Marina.

"He might be for you."

"I'm no cougar," Gilda said with a sigh. "Though I sometimes wish I were. Well, a woman can always enjoy a nice view."

Marina laughed and moved on. A few minutes later, she returned, satisfied that Heather, Ethan, and the other servers hired for the event were doing well.

After appetizers were served, everyone gathered for dinner at the tables on the inn's large patio. It wasn't the largest or most elaborate wedding, but it was an intimate group of good friends who were truly happy for the couple. As the setting sun cast golden hues across the scene, Marina thought she had never seen a prettier beach wedding.

Leo was sitting with his mother and her new husband. Also at their table were Vanessa's good friends, Denise and John Davis, and their daughter Samantha, who was Leo's best friend. They were like family to Leo because he'd grown up next door to them, and Vanessa and Denise were as close as sisters. When Vanessa moved to Summer Beach, the family followed, and John started a technology consulting practice.

Kai was seated with Ginger, and the first course of cold avocado gazpacho was being served. Jack and Axe, the broad-shouldered contractor who'd built the Seashell amphitheater, were talking to Mayor Bennett at another table. Marina saw Kai motion to them.

Axe also had a beautiful baritone voice. Over the last year, he and Kai had collaborated on their theater-under-the-stars experience, which was a welcome addition to Summer Beach. The two had a symbiotic professional partnership and were very much in love. With her background as a musical theater performer, Kai was eager to write and direct.

Marina had a part in the holiday production last year. However, she preferred working behind the scenes, supplying the picnic box dinners. And soon, a new food truck experience, she hoped.

As Marina took her seat, she turned to Kai. "How's your new production going? You've been rehearsing late almost every night. Will you be ready for opening night this week?"

Kai beamed. "Of course, and it's going to be spectacular."

Her sister and Axe had written a new musical, *Belles on the Beach*. Marina had heard Kai humming some new tunes, and she wondered if those were in the show. "I wish you'd let us sit in on a rehearsal." Evidently, the actors had all been sworn to secrecy.

"Absolutely not." Kai's eyes sparkled with delight. "It's

meant to be a surprise. But I will say that it's a very feel-good story."

"When I rose from my nap," Ginger began, turning to Marina. "I saw a food truck in front of the cafe. Bright yellow and awfully hard to miss. Was that a friend of yours?"

With a quick smile, Marina replied, "I wanted it to be a surprise, but that kitchen-on-wheels might soon be part of the Coral Cafe. If it checks out, I'll buy it. I've been shopping around, and I know the owner is giving me a great deal."

"What a perfectly marvelous idea." Delight filled Ginger's face. "Oh, the places we can take that. What fun we'll have."

Marina loved that Ginger was always up for an adventure, even at her age. "It's a shame, but the yellow submarine theme will have to go. It has to be branded with the Coral Cafe colors and logo."

"Maybe Jack could help with that," Ginger suggested. "He's so talented."

"I know you're his number one fan, but I have an experienced graphic designer who can do that," Marina said lightly. She liked directing her business on her own.

"As long as we're talking about surprises, I have one for you, too." Kai leaned toward Marina, lowering her voice. "I shouldn't be telling you this, but word is getting around town about you and Jack."

"Now what? Do we have a secret baby or something?" Marina asked, only half in jest. Gossip was a popular pastime in Summer Beach.

Kai flipped her hand. "No one ever believed that silly rumor. But seriously, I saw Jack shopping in the village. He asked me not to say anything, and I haven't, but I wasn't the only one there, if you know what I mean."

"Why would shopping be a big deal?"

"It's what he was looking at." Kai discreetly tapped the bare ring finger on Marina's left hand. On hers, Kai was wearing an engagement ring Axe had given her. Kai loved unusual pieces, and hers was a vintage ruby ring she planned to wear with thin wedding bands of different gemstones as the whim took her.

Marina's heart skipped a beat at the thought, yet she wasn't entirely sure she and Jack were ready. And she was surprised that her sister would bring this up. She pressed a hand down. "I don't want to hear this right now."

"I didn't want to spoil the surprise, but I figured you're going to hear it sooner or later, so it might as well be from me." Kai wrinkled her nose. "Please don't be mad at me."

Marina pressed a hand against her sister's forearm, swallowing her guarded excitement. "Are you sure?"

"I was there. And you know what it means when a man goes shopping." Kai gave her a pointed look. "Women shop as a fun excursion. Even if we don't buy anything, we'll have lunch or coffee. But for men, shopping is a mission. They aim to slap down that credit card and seize the goods." Kai bounced in her chair. "Aren't you a little excited?"

Marina was, but not like Kai would expect. "I'm not like you. This isn't my first time."

"You can still be excited."

"I am. Really." Marina had a more mature outlook than Kai. She was older, but she'd also been through much more than her sister. "I'm more concerned about making the right decision this time."

Kai arched an eyebrow. She wasn't leaving this alone. "Didn't you mention that Jack had made a reservation at Beaches?"

As soon as her sister said that, a picture developed in her mind. Was that why he'd made so sure that she had that date available? He'd been casual about it, but he'd also asked her three times. That was very unlike Jack.

"Several weeks ago," Marina admitted. "Reservations are hard to get in the summer."

"That's it," Kai cried in triumph, thrusting her hand in the air.

"*Yeesy Louisey*, keep it down." Marina shushed her with an old expression she'd once used around the twins when they were young. It had stuck with her, just like *easy, peasy, cheesy*.

Kai lowered her voice to a stage whisper again. "I'll bet he pops the question there. After all, it's the most romantic restaurant in Summer Beach."

Marina blinked at the possibility. Jack had made a point of telling her that he'd reserved one of the best tables with an ocean view precisely at sunset. Now she realized he'd have to check to make sure exactly what time the sun set. While Jack had that exacting attention to detail in him, it was usually reserved for his professional work. In his regular day-to-day life, he often operated at the remedial level, which made them both laugh. If he were a teacher, he'd be the quintessential absent-minded professor.

Though a much better-looking one. Jack's thick, unruly hair and deep blue eyes that blazed with intellect had attracted her, almost unwillingly at first. And his runs on the beach with Bennett were certainly enhancing an already nice physique.

A frisson of excitement gathered in her chest. Had Jack decided to propose? More than that, was she ready for this step? They would have much to talk about first. Marina exhaled to calm her sudden jitters.

"Well? What do you think? Won't this be fun with both of us getting married?" Kai peppered her with questions.

Marina had to laugh. "You might be in the starry-eyed phase of love, but I know the other facets of marriage. Not that it isn't worth it—it's just that my eyes are open." Still, she longed for that deep connection again.

Tossing her mane of strawberry blond hair across a shoulder, Kai pressed her again. "Oh, come on. It's totally worth it. Just be a little excited—for me? It took everything I had not to tell you. But Darla at Java Beach is talking about it, and you know what that means. I think you and Jack are absolutely perfect together."

Ginger watched her granddaughters with a bemused smile, quietly sipping a glass of wine.

"Perfect?" Marina swept her hands apart. "That doesn't exist. But at this stage of my life, a relationship will have to be as right as two flawed human beings can manage. Perfection is over-rated and far too stressful."

That was her logical side speaking. She recalled with fondness how she and Stan had laughed at their silly mishaps. And with Jack, they had plenty of laughs, too.

Now transfixed with the growing thought, Marina gazed across the patio at Jack, his profile illuminated by a string of overhead lights that cast a soft glow. As practical as she was trying to be, just seeing him made her heart leap like a teenager's.

She'd grown to love Jack, but was he a forever sort of man? And was that a chance she was willing to take?

With a soft sigh, she brought her attention back to the table.

Ginger was staring at Marina and Kai with a small smile playing on her lips. "I had a feeling about you and Jack. After all, it seems summer weddings are in the air. Even if we don't know the exact dates."

Their grandmother was also referring to Kai, who had decided to move up her wedding to this summer. Kai might have divulged Jack's secret, but she wouldn't share why she and Axe had moved up their wedding from the spring of next year, other than to say that she preferred a summer wedding. Marina wondered if that was the truth, especially since it was the high summer season.

Marina gave a self-conscious laugh. "Maybe Jack is simply treating me to a nice dinner to make up for the last fiasco there."

She and Jack seldom went out because she did most of the

cooking. Usually, Jack and Leo showed up at the cafe. Sometimes he asked her to make dinner at his house after she closed the cafe, though she was often tired. Frankly, she would have liked a good meal after serving others all day.

However, Marina knew something had shifted in their relationship. Tonight, he'd clutched her hand so tightly during the ceremony. Emotional tears had filled his eyes.

Was he thinking about the future of their relationship?

Catching her breath, she grinned at Kai and Ginger. Maybe this was really happening.

2

*J*ack was running out of time. After Vanessa's wedding last week, he realized he needed to make a decision about a ring. Even if Marina didn't like what he chose, they could return it. But he'd made enough promises and empty allusions to their future. This time, he was committed. Now, he had to make sure she knew it.

With a surreptitious glance behind him worthy of a spy, he ducked into another jewelry shop in the village. Plenty of dolphin necklaces, starfish earrings, and beach-inspired charm bracelets dangled from displays and filled cases, but that's what you gave a girlfriend.

Not the woman you planned to marry. If she'd have him, that is.

He let out a nervous breath and popped one of those curiously strong mints into his mouth. He'd been buying them in bulk ever since he stopped smoking to quell his nerves whenever he felt the urge to backslide. His first editor had been a chain smoker, and he'd picked up the habit on late-night deadlines.

He drew a breath, focusing on the bracing peppermint and the life he imagined with Marina and Leo.

Seeing Vanessa and Dr. Noah pledge themselves to one another had been so beautiful and touching. Their marriage meant a great deal to Leo. After all, Dr. Noah's medical discovery saved his mother's life.

Jack knew how much his son loved Marina, too. He couldn't mess this up.

Turning, Jack spied a glass case that held wedding bands and engagement rings. Resting his hands on the edges, he peered inside, trying to act nonchalant. Still, his heart was hammering.

The shopkeeper moved toward him. "Anything I can help you with?"

The tall woman had a beachy look. Silver-palm trees dangled from her earlobes, and her sundress had a similar pattern.

"This case looks sort of interesting."

A knowing look curved the woman's mouth. "I can show you anything you like here."

Jack scanned the assortment, but nothing jumped out at him. Nothing that was as unique as Marina. At the mere thought of her, his chest tightened in the once unfamiliar way that he'd grown accustomed to now.

As a young man, he recalled his father pressing a hand to his chest, saying that he didn't know how to describe love, but he knew it was real because he felt it every time he looked at his wife.

Jack rubbed a hand on his chest. He had that feeling now —and every time he saw Marina.

At the Coral Cottage, he'd seen her wedding photo displayed on one of Ginger's bookcases. She had worn a slim band and a simple patterned dress. The only giveaway was the bouquet she carried and the good-looking young man who stood beaming beside her in a uniform.

Jack had been struck by her youth and beauty, although in his eyes, Marina was even more beautiful now. She had maturity, sophistication, and intelligence. A powerful package, indeed. But most of all, he loved her for what was in her heart, for the way she cared for her family and friends. And for him and Leo.

He smiled to himself. Even Scout was smitten.

The woman unlocked the glass cabinet. "I'll show you our most popular rings."

With a second look at the counter, he quickly decided there was nothing here that was special enough for her. He twisted his mouth to one side. "You have some nice pieces, but I'm looking for something different. One of a kind."

The woman nodded. "Like her, right?"

Jack's face grew warm. "Guess you've heard that before."

"Maybe we can accommodate you. We have a relationship with an excellent designer who visits Summer Beach often. Elena Eaton has an amazing line, and she accepts special commissions. Her upscale boutique on Robertson Boulevard in Los Angeles is a gorgeous little jewel box, and a lot of Hollywood stars wear her pieces. Some of her work was in *Vogue* magazine just last month." The woman picked up a photo binder from a display behind her and began to flip through it.

That sounded interesting to Jack. He leaned forward to inspect photos of glittery rings and bracelets with a rainbow of stones. "Wow. That's a lot of gemstones."

"Fancy-colored diamonds are her specialty."

"Does she do anything, uh…"

The woman must have read his mind because she flipped to the back of the book, where more simple designs were showcased. The stones were still fairly large, and now that he had Leo, likely out of his budget.

Besides, he was saving for an important goal. The illustrations for Ginger's books had brought in a modest advance. At his beach rental, he was subletting the old artist's studio above his garage by the week, mostly to surfers and young people piling in for a beach vacation. He was also writing a few articles for a magazine back east. He wanted to share this goal with Marina at Beaches. And a lot more.

Jack shook his head. "These are nice, but not quite right."

"As I said, she does custom work. What's your lead time?"

"I'm not sure. Soon, I hope."

"Elena Eaton is backed up about six months for custom pieces."

"Six months?" he echoed. But she was talented. A real artist, in fact.

"At least. Many people plan weddings pretty far ahead."

Jack ran a hand through his hair and gave a self-conscious grin. "That's never been my style. But she does incredible work. Thanks for showing me. What's her connection with Summer Beach?"

"Elena has family here. She's part of the Bay family."

Jack nodded in thought. "Would one of them be Ivy Bay at the Seabreeze Inn?"

"Sure is. That's her aunt. Do you know her?"

"I've stayed there in the past." Jack grinned. Summer Beach was a small town, and he didn't want word to get around that he was ring shopping. Ivy was an old friend of Marina's. It seemed like everyone in town knew Marina or Ivy —or both of them. He'd run into Kai at a shop last week, but he'd sworn her to secrecy, confident that she'd keep her word.

"Anything else I can show you?"

"Not today, thanks."

After another glance before stepping outside, Jack hurried toward the Coral Cafe. It was almost lunchtime.

Maybe he should have done this ring shopping before, even last Christmas as Axe had. But at that time, he hadn't exactly proposed.

Or had he? After one of the holiday performances at the Seashell last season, *A Christmas Carol…at the Beach*, he remembered saying to Marina, *Merry Christmas, Mrs. Cratchit, but I'd rather say Ventana.*

Did that count as a proposal? He'd also told her he wanted a life together—and he intended to keep that promise. Now, with Kai and Axe having moved up their wedding, Jack was feeling the pressure.

And it wasn't all coming from him. He'd sensed a change in Marina, too. Especially after Vanessa's wedding. A woman like her could have almost anyone she wanted, even if she didn't believe that. If he truly wanted to spend his life with her, he needed to make his intention known.

Because if he didn't, someone else would. Now, since he was no longer in a dangerous, widow-maker line of work, he could make and keep a promise to a woman. In the past, he'd always left before breaking their hearts too badly, sparing them the possibility of devastating grief. He quickened his pace.

Marina wasn't just any woman. She had become every-thing to him. Until now, Jack had never known how deeply he could care for someone. That made him feel at once both vulnerable and superhuman. It didn't make sense, but he felt stronger with her by his side, though she could crush him with a word if she chose.

She would be working today, of course. The beachside restaurant was doing a brisk business now, but just being near her made him happy.

After lunch, Leo's mother would drop him off. Jack and Leo would go to the beach, which his son never tired of doing. Later, they'd stop by the cafe for dinner, too. Leo had already voiced his opinion on Jack's lack of culinary talent. Jack laughed as he thought of that. Leo had opened his heart, too.

As Jack recalled how driven and calloused he had once been, he also reflected on how lonely he had been. Now, he hardly recognized himself in this new life, but he liked it. And he never wanted it to end.

However, a decision like this one with Marina took a lot

more courage than he realized. Still, he was ready. A few weeks ago, he had reserved a table at Beaches for the occasion. He wanted this date to be everything that Marina deserved.

As he swung out into the sunshine, his gaze fell on another little shop, Antique Times. They had a section for pre-owned jewelry there.

A thought crossed his mind. Would Marina like a vintage ring?

Suddenly, another idea sprang to mind. Reaching into his pocket, Jack pulled out his phone. He hadn't told his sister how serious he was about Marina yet. Liz had once complained that she couldn't keep up with his revolving door.

His sister answered on the first ring, and her Texas drawl was quickly evident. "Well, hey, stranger. How're you doin'?"

"Great. Miss me?" They had an easy relationship, even though they didn't talk often. She was usually busy with her children, and Jack had been on the road in one time zone or another for years.

She laughed. "I don't have time to miss you. But I still do, you old goat."

They talked while Jack walked from the village toward the Coral Cafe. "You and Ryder should bring the kids to the beach this summer."

Liz laughed. "Is that an invitation?"

"Actually, it is. I've got that restored VW van the kids could sleep in. It's pretty nice inside and has a little kitchenette. They'd have fun camping in the driveway and walking to the beach. You might not even see them that much."

"Aw, you're just trying to sweet talk me now."

"I know how to get to an overworked mom's heart." He chuckled along with her. "But seriously, it would be great to see you all. I know it's easier for me to visit, but I think I'm going to have an important occasion this summer. And I need a favor from you."

Quickly, he told her what he had in mind.

Liz listened. "Marina sounds special. I don't think I've ever heard you talk about a woman like this."

"Guess I finally grew up. I've been pretty shallow, haven't I?"

"I wouldn't say that. You had a lot to contribute and accomplish. I've always been proud of you and what you've done. Not many people win a Pulitzer Prize, at least not in my neck of the woods, though you'll always be my baby brother. Just wish Mom and Dad were still around to hear this news."

"So do I." Jack still missed his parents. They were gone too young from a life of hard work, though they had loved farming, like Liz and her husband. "You'll get to meet Leo. He's been asking about his cousins."

They talked a little more, then Liz said, "I'll look through Mom's things for you right away and talk to Ryder. We have neighbors down the road who could look after the livestock while we're gone."

"That would be great." Jack turned toward the cafe.

After he hung up, he strolled to the open-air cafe and spotted Heather, Marina's daughter. She was a younger version of her mother, though Jack knew her misty gray-blue eyes came from her father. Her golden, dark blond hair was wound into a knot at the nape of her neck. She wore a tank top, cotton capris, and an apron emblazoned with the logo and words, *Coral Cafe*.

That was new. Jack admired how adept Marina was at branding her business.

He eased out a chair at his regular table on the large patio where he could watch Marina in the kitchen. Locals and tourists were gathered around tables shaded by coral canvas umbrellas. The mood was as bright as the sunshine.

"Hey, Jack." Heather pushed aside the reserved sign on the table and gave him a broad grin. "What'll it be today?"

"I don't know, what day is it?" Working for himself, he

often lost track of the days unless he had Leo. Marina rotated certain items on the menu for the locals.

Heather laughed. "It's New England clam chowder day."

"Then I'll have that with a salad."

"Is that all?"

"I'm saving my appetite for supper." Leo was at Samantha's house now, but he'd pick him up later.

Heather was a good kid—a young woman, he corrected himself. She attended college in San Diego. They got along well, although he could feel the reservations that her brother Ethan still had about him. It wasn't anything he'd actually said, and they got on pretty well, too, but Jack figured Ethan was looking out for his mother. As a young man should.

Heather put a glass of water in front of him. "Okay, one clam chowder and a house salad, coming right up. We'll have Leo's favorite chocolate chunk ice cream tonight."

"That's mine, too." Marina made her own ice cream for the cafe. It was decadent, but as long as he kept running with the mayor in the morning, he could indulge. The question was if he could keep up with Bennett.

A large party of out-of-towners walked in, and Jack nodded toward them. "You see to them. I'll put in my order with the chef. Won't hurt your tip, I promise."

Heather let out a breath. "Thanks. It's been super busy today. We were slammed the minute we opened this morning, and it hasn't let up."

After Heather left to tend to the large group, Jack looked around the patio. The tourists outnumbered the locals, so he didn't see too many familiar faces. Everyone seemed to be having a good time. He made his way toward the kitchen, which had once been the guest house he'd stayed in when he first arrived in Summer Beach. During the renovation, Marina had installed doors that opened wide, allowing her to see the patio while she cooked.

Marina glanced up when she saw him coming, and a smile lit her face. "You're late today."

"Had to run a few errands in town." He leaned against the chef's table on the other side of the counter, admiring her. She wore a floral-print chef jacket, and she moved with swift efficiency. The younger man was a tattooed surfer nicknamed Cruise, and he was tending to the sweet potato fries, which were turning crisp. They smelled delicious.

"Heather is with a large group, so I told her I'd deliver my order to you."

As she plated crab cakes, she gestured to the side. "I've got your chowder today."

"You read my mind. Along with a salad and some of those fries." He paused, wishing he could help, but cooking had never been one of his talents, unless it was on a grill. He could grow the food, but what happened to it in the kitchen was often a mystery to him. Growing up, his mother and sister had cooked while he and his father tended the farm.

Still, Jack wished he could ease her burden. He didn't know how she did it, being on her feet all day, but she seemed to love what she did. "Can I bus tables or something? I'm good at dishes."

Marina laughed. "We'll let you know if we need you. Do you want your chowder now?"

"I'll wait. See you later."

Jack walked from the kitchen and turned toward the restroom access off the back of the building. A whispered conversation floated toward him from around the corner. His old instinct for news kicked in, and he paused to listen.

"This is a dump of a town. This is the kind of place the government sticks people to disappear."

Jack held his breath. Probably someone making a tired joke. The speaker's voice and his words didn't quite align for this to be real. Personally, he liked the small community; it was a welcome change from New York and Chicago—and a couple of other foreign countries where he'd literally been in the line of fire.

"No way is he in a witness protection program. He's using his real name, I tell you."

Despite his doubts, Jack's curiosity surged.

"Or he's on a story. Must be a big one. He's gone to a lot of trouble to make himself blend in. A kid, a dog."

At once, a shiver sliced through him. A lot of people in town had kids and dogs. But how many of them wrote? Still, he didn't know everyone.

"I don't think it's his kid. Never listed in his bio, and this one's older."

A cold sweat covered him. The guy sounded young, and he might be talking about Leo. Jack had to see who this was. Could he risk it? He inched closer to the edge.

"Yeah, yeah. I got this. Later."

Jack lurched around the corner, but the guy was rounding the corner in the other direction. *Jeans, brown hair. Dark shirt.* Just then, the bathroom door opened in his path. He nearly slammed into it.

"Oh, hey, Jack," came Jen's chirpy voice. She and her husband owned a hardware shop in the village. "What are you doing lurking around here like James Bond?" She stepped in front of him.

Jack pressed his hands downward, signaling her to lower her voice. With a nimble step, he dodged her, leaving her with her mouth ajar.

Careening toward the other side of the building, he scanned the area.

No one.

He whipped around. *Where'd he go?*

He turned back to the kitchen. Marina was still working at breakneck speed.

"Hey," he said amiably, approaching her. "I just missed a friend. Did you see anyone come this way?"

Marina shook her head. "Heather has your order."

Jack stared at Cruise. It couldn't have been him. He'd been here all along by the deep fryer. Same jeans and a black T-shirt, but a long apron over it all.

Turning back toward the patio, he scanned the crowd for other guys in jeans. One, two, three...there were quite a lot of them. Some were leaving. He whirled around, but there was no one out front either. The man was a veritable Houdini.

Heather was putting his lunch on the table. "Enjoy."

"Did you see a guy come by in jeans and a dark shirt? Probably a T-shirt."

"I haven't noticed. A friend of yours?"

"I'm not sure. Will you let me know?"

Heather swept a hand over her forehead and glanced over her shoulder. "It's pretty busy, but if I see someone like that, I'll send him your way." With that, she hurried toward another table.

Jack stared at his food. Had he heard that conversation correctly?

Feeling frustrated, he made his way back to the restrooms but couldn't see anything unusual. After returning to his table, he ate quickly and left a generous amount on the table for Heather before leaving.

In the span of a minute or so, his mood had swiftly changed. As he walked home, he glanced around, but he saw nothing out of the ordinary. The sun was shimmering on the waves, people were laughing and playing volleyball on the beach, and boats were easing out of the marina.

Jack climbed the steps to his cottage and opened the door. He checked the house, then opened the back door and whistled. Scout bounded toward him with his awkward gait, probably the result of an injury as a young puppy before Jack had adopted him. He knelt and scratched the yellow Labrador retriever's ears. "See anything, bud?"

Scout tossed his head back and forth and wagged his tail.

"No? That's good. You'll tell me if you do, right?"

Jack grabbed a stick and threw it across the yard. Scout bounded after it, narrowly missing low-hanging lemons and oranges.

He'd been meaning to trim those trees before they flowered, but the fruit was too good to waste now. Scout would have to deal with it. But then, he liked playing with the fruit, too. Silly old dog.

Jack went back inside to his studio off the bedroom where he worked. Built as a sunroom, the light was perfect for the illustrations he was doing for Ginger's series of children's books. He sat down and stared from the window. He had a little time before Leo arrived.

Outside, the scene was as innocuous as it could be. This was Summer Beach, after all. Not much went on here except for the yacht incident last year. That was a one-off situation, and certainly not related to what he'd overheard.

He picked up a pencil and went to work. By the time he'd completed his drawing, a knock sounded on the door, and he could hear Leo stomping on the front porch, eager to go to the beach. And Jack had nearly finished talking himself out of what he'd overhead.

After all, this was Summer Beach.

3

*M*arina loved early mornings at the beach, though today, thoughts had been zinging through her mind like comets even before the sun rose. As she lay in bed in the half-light deciding whether to get up or go back to sleep, she rubbed her ring finger and wondered if Jack was really going through with what she suspected. Their date was tonight.

She'd tossed half the night thinking about what Kai had confided at the wedding, her feelings vacillating like a pendulum between nervous excitement and guarded trepidation.

Rising from her old iron bed, she thought about the busy week ahead. *Potentially life-changing date, Kai's bridal shower, food truck purchase, opening night at the Seashell.* What had she forgotten?

Oh, yes. Baking for the farmers market stand Brooke managed.

Quickly, she rifled through her armoire stuffed with faded sundresses, jeans, and T-shirts—and far too many conservative outfits from her on-air anchor job. Marina selected a short black dress that would have to do for tonight, even if it wasn't terribly flattering anymore. Owning a cafe could be hazardous to the waistline. She set it aside.

For now, she pulled on a T-shirt, joggers, and a hoodie. As she dressed, she thought of her youngest sister. Kai's bridal shower had been changed to this week. Her theater friends from New York and Los Angeles were arriving soon, along with friends from Summer Beach.

Marina had been shopping and making preparations for the week ahead. She had a great deal of work in the kitchen and needed to clear her mind before she began.

Taking care not to wake Kai, Ginger, or Heather, Marina tiptoed downstairs, avoiding the wooden planks on the stairs that creaked the loudest, and slowly opened the squeaky front door.

The cool sea breeze misted her face. After her parents had died in an auto accident when she was eighteen, she'd often escaped to the beach, watching the sunrise and thinking about them. The bracing ocean breeze helped soothe her spirits, even when she had been at her lowest.

Now, although she was on the verge of a bright future, she was still nervous. She blinked against the wind as she set off in the direction of the Seabreeze Inn. Her friend Ivy would be busy preparing breakfast for the early risers. Maybe they could talk later. She needed the advice of a good friend—or Ginger, who was the wisest person she knew.

Marina zipped up her hoodie. Today, her life might change forever.

Since last Christmas, she and Jack had seen each other nearly every day, but tonight would be different. She hardly dared to imagine what he would say. Though recently, Jack had been alluding to—and then avoiding—the issue of their future.

Thinking about this, she fidgeted with a thread in the pocket of her hoodie before realizing she'd made a hole in it.

Marina blew out a breath. She had to get a grip on herself.

At any age, this was a major step. She'd been widowed for two decades, and Jack had never been married. It was only natural to be nervous about formalizing a new life together.

Right?

Still fidgeting, she made the hole larger and stuck her little finger through it. She kicked a piece of driftwood back into the sea.

Yet, she could hardly wait for tonight. Every time she thought of Jack, a sense of belonging suffused her limbs with a tingly warmth she couldn't quite describe—a feeling she hadn't known since her first husband.

She longed to start fresh with Jack. He might not be perfect—neither was she—but they had so much in common, beginning with their interest in news reporting, although they'd both left that profession for Summer Beach. And they both adored Leo, of course, Jack's recently discovered young son. Jack was good with her children, too. He ticked all the boxes, but more than that, their relationship simply felt right.

Marina sidestepped a pair of low-flying white gulls coming in for a beach landing.

"Watch where you're going, silly."

She caught herself. *Who talked to birds?* She'd heard of people who withdrew from society, preferring the company of wild animals. Sometimes after a long shift at the cafe, that seemed terribly appealing.

Was she really ready for a 24/7 relationship?

Something else Kai had said grated against her nerves as well. *If you marry Jack, your life will change again someday. No way will that man be happy in Summer Beach forever.*

Did Kai see a thirst in Jack that she had missed?

But then, they weren't actually engaged. Not formally, anyway. And that's what Marina wanted, even if it seemed old-fashioned, especially at her age. She wanted to know where she stood with him so they could plan their future together.

She loved Jack, and she knew what her heart yearned for, but if she was being honest with herself, was she ready for the responsibility of a somewhat disorganized new husband and his son, along with an overgrown puppy?

Less than two years ago, every element in her life had been dumped from the box like a puzzle; the pieces fit better now, but the image was still developing. Marina was no stranger to upheaval, yet she had other considerations as well.

Twice in her life, her grandmother's home had become her sanctuary. Still, she couldn't live there forever, even with her cafe on the property. She needed a place of her own.

Their own.

Stretching her arms overhead, Marina gazed toward the cliffs cocooning Summer Beach in a rocky embrace. She loved it here, but was this beach village too safe? Was Kai right about the novelty of a small-town life wearing off for Jack? He'd been an investigative reporter at the top of his game when he landed here. She'd been fairly confident about the trajectory of their relationship until Kai's astute observation.

How had Marina missed that?

She blew wisps of hair from her face. Dawn was tossing pink streamers through a powder-blue sky, and the sun was cresting the ridgetop with a halo of light. Even in the summer, a cool morning breeze blew off the ocean toward the beach, filling the air with a salty, briny mixture that was forever etched in her memory. She'd spent a large part of her childhood at her grandmother's beloved Coral Cottage.

As she turned to face the sea crashing toward her, she pulled her cotton hoodie over her head and then skipped back from the rushing water as she had as a child. Only now, she had grown-up issues nagging at her.

Just as she trotted into the strong, receding surf, a yellow Labrador retriever bounded toward her with an awkward loping gait. Splashing in the water's edge, the dog jumped to greet her, its tongue lolling from its mouth with what looked like a perpetual grin.

"Hey, Scout." She laughed at the exuberant dog, whose sandy paws marked her white cotton joggers. She didn't care. "Where's your sidekick?"

Behind her, she heard a whistle.

Jack and Bennett were jogging toward her on the beach. While she knew the mayor ran early, she was surprised to see Jack. He wore a faded T-shirt with the words *New York Times*, one of his former employers. His thick brown hair stuck up in all directions, and a dark stubble peppered his jaw.

Her heart quickened at the sight of him.

"You're up early." She greeted Jack with a quick morning kiss while Scout wagged his wet tail, joyfully slapping it against their legs.

"Had to make a few early phone calls back east, so I decided to meet up with Bennett." Jack tucked a windblown strand of hair behind her ear. "Didn't think you'd be out here either."

"I couldn't sleep." She wondered if Jack was feeling the same excitement about tonight. Feeling a little nervous, she glanced down—only to see his taut, muscular legs extending from his running shorts.

Catching her gaze, Jack grinned and tugged the edge of the fabric. "Too short?"

"No one cares," Bennett said, still running in place. "Unless I wore them. Then I'd never hear the end of it around town. Or at Java Beach."

Marina angled her chin toward the coffee shop that spilled onto the beach. "I'm headed there as soon as Mitch opens. I didn't want to wake the household."

"Isn't it nice to have someone wait on you for a change?" A grin lit Jack's face.

Bennett chuckled. "Sounds like there's a job opening for you, old man."

"Get out of here." Jack nudged him.

He was a little too quick to answer, Marina thought. Maybe Jack was feeling self-conscious. Or unsure of himself. This was a huge step for both of them.

"Go on, get your run in," she said. "I just saw Mitch pull into Java Beach."

"And here comes Ginger." Squinting ahead, Jack gestured behind her in the direction of the cottage.

Marina sighed lightly. "I must have woken her after all." She'd tried to slip out of the house, but the creak of the wooden door must have given her away. Turning, she waved at Ginger. "Tell her I'll wait for her if she wants to join me for a coffee at Mitch's."

"Will do. If I have time, I'll bring Leo for lunch later. Unless something comes up."

"I'll be there."

As she always was. She often wondered if she was too dependable and too available. The forty-something girlfriend who lived with the grandmother, although she hadn't been back in Summer Beach very long. She didn't have the ticking of a child-bearing clock like Kai. Still, she wanted more. If she was going to build a life with a partner, she wanted to get on with it.

This was their time.

Just then, Jack's phone buzzed, and he pulled it from his pocket. As he read it, a deep frown creased his face.

"Trouble?"

"Probably nothing," he muttered, shutting off his phone. With a scowl, he shoved it back into his pocket.

Marina wondered what that was all about. Scout circled him, sniffing his ankles. The dog seemed inquisitive as well. She bent to scratch Scout behind his ears.

"See you later then." Jack gave her an absent-minded peck on the cheek. Before starting off with Bennett, he flashed a grin, but he still seemed distracted by whatever message had come across his phone.

Yet at his simple touch, Marina's heart thumped. If Jack wasn't the one, then her man-picker was broken. She hadn't felt like this since she'd met her first husband, Stan.

With a last yelp at her, Scout bounded off with the guys, quickly pulling ahead of them.

She and Jack would have a long talk tonight at Beaches, she decided. The last time she'd been there was with an old friend, Cole Beaufort. Unfortunately, Scout had bounded inside and interrupted her dinner date in a spectacular fashion.

They could laugh about that now. Jack had decided she needed a do-over at Beaches with him. She blew out a breath. Maybe that's all this was about.

As Marina watched the two friends jog away from her, she waved at her grandmother and started walking toward her. Marina's thoughts turned back to Kai and Axe. While touring on the theater circuit for years, her sister had tried to date, but it had been difficult to maintain relationships when she didn't spend much time in any place.

Marina's mind reeled back—where had the years gone? Falling in love in her twenties had been so different than it was now. Not that she'd been carefree then. If not for Ginger, Marina didn't know what she and her two younger sisters would have done without their parents. Her grandmother had been there for them. And for Marina again when Stan died.

There were times when her children were younger that Marina wondered if she should remarry to give the kids a chance at having a life with two parents. But between her grief over Stan and the demands of caring for two active youngsters—which she couldn't have done without Ginger— she hadn't been in the psychological space to even notice a man, let alone find much time to date, with one disastrous exception that had sent her life into a tailspin. Now that

Heather and Ethan were making their way in the world, it was her turn again.

Marina slowed to a stop and hugged Ginger. "Good morning. I hope I didn't wake you."

"Nonsense. I was already up. I suppose you have a lot on your mind. Want to talk about it?"

"You know I do." Ginger always saw the solutions to problems so clearly. "Where shall I start? The food truck or Jack?"

"Both are crucial decisions. One you can control, one you can't." Ginger gave her a sidelong glance, seeming to gauge her mood. "Tell me about your plans for the truck first."

Momentarily relieved, Marina let her pragmatic side take over. "I've already scheduled a mechanic and inspection service. If the vehicle and the interior systems check out, I'll test my concept at the Seashell for opening night of Kai's new production."

"I trust you've created a business plan for this?"

"I have. A food truck is a simple concept on the surface, but there are a lot of details to tend to. Insurance, maintenance, staffing, and a streamlined menu. I've got the expense and food cost side figured out."

Ginger nodded thoughtfully. "How will you reach your customers?"

"I've researched and created a calendar of local events in and near Summer Beach, and I found a website and app where I can include my truck and post where I'll be. I can send out a newsletter to my best customers."

Ginger looked at her with admiration. "Those are excellent ideas. But do you know anyone with a food truck?"

"I have a friend in the Bay Area who operates a Thai noodle truck, and she's created a very good business. She suggested opportunities I hadn't thought about and reviewed my projected financials. I also reviewed the plan with my accountant and banker."

Marina had a team of trusted advisors now, although the

decisions were still hers. Just talking about this project helped her organize her thoughts. Maybe that's what Ginger had in mind.

"Sounds like you developed a solid plan." Ginger rubbed Marina's shoulder with pride. "You've become quite a good businesswoman."

"Thanks, but starting the cafe was a sink or swim proposition, wasn't it?"

"Regardless, you created a goal and rose to the challenge. As traumatic as being fired from a position can be, that experience opened a window to a brand-new world. It's as if the universe prodded you to find your true purpose. I'd say you found yours." Ginger's eyes twinkled. "For now, anyway. Life is a book full of chapters."

"I suppose that advice goes for relationships, too."

"Of course. Some relationships are short stories, some are sagas." Ginger patted her hand. "Now, tell me about Jack."

"I'm not sure about our story." As they walked on the beach, and Marina opened up to Ginger, she realized her relationship with Jack was still a work-in-progress. As exciting as Kai's news had been, she wasn't entirely sure what she would do.

4

a knock sounded at Jack's door, and he pushed away from his sketch pad to investigate. As he stood, his muscles ached from his early run.

This time, he paused to look out a window first, not something he'd ever felt he had to do in Summer Beach. Scout padded behind him, curious about his actions.

He hadn't been able to get that conversation he'd overheard at the cafe out of his mind. While he'd known that the investigative reporting he'd done could pose future threats, he didn't have a family back then.

Peering through a slit in the blinds, Jack saw a postal van pull away. *All clear.*

He'd never been much concerned for his safety, and he'd been in plenty of dangerous situations working on crucial stories. But now, he had Leo to think about. The boy was playing video games in his bedroom.

Jack unlocked the door and collected the box resting on his porch. It was from his sister in Texas. Liz had wasted no time finding what he asked for and sending it to him. He tore open the box. A faded red velvet box tumbled out, along with a host of memories.

His grandmother Josephine had worn this ring most of her life. She had been a proud, hard-working woman who forged a future for her family and her descendants. In many ways, Marina reminded him of his grandmother.

Grandma Josephine was whip-smart, practical, and forward-thinking. As a young woman growing up on a Texas farm, Josephine had dreamed of more, even though opportunities for women were limited back then. Yet, through sheer determination, she became an entrepreneur, designing fine clothes for women. She sold her first pieces to the upscale Neiman Marcus department store and traveled by rail to hold trunk shows at other exclusive boutiques in New York, Chicago, Kansas City, San Francisco, Seattle, and Los Angeles.

In Dallas, she met his grandfather, a newspaperman. And that was how Jack had come by his fascination for news, even though his father and mother had preferred working the family farm, as hard as it was.

As Jack opened the velvet box, the tarnished hinges creaked with age. Nestled inside was a heavy platinum band with a double row of old, European-cut diamonds. It wasn't flashy, but it was of the finest quality. Just the sort of ring that Marina could wear even while she worked in the kitchen if she wanted.

The ring had come just in time for his dinner with Marina.

As he was admiring the craftsmanship, his phone buzzed in his pocket. His former editor's name flashed across the screen. *Gus Gustafson.* He'd called this morning, too, but Jack hadn't answered it, and he'd forgotten to call him back. He tapped his phone.

"Hey, Gus. How goes it at the *Daily Salt Mine?*"

"We are just waxing nostalgic about one of our most prominent escapees. Has the sun fried your brain yet?"

Jack chuckled. "Only around the edges. But the sea breeze is good for clearing the cobwebs."

"What's this about you illustrating children's books? Tell me we've got that wrong. You've always been a hard-news man."

"Times change, Gus."

"I know you, Jack. That's why I'm calling. Some new information just crossed my desk. Thought you'd want to know." He brought up a name from the past.

Jack remembered all too well. White-collar criminal with mob ties. Money laundering. A suave character on the outside but ruthless on the inside. His investigative reporting had broken the story and led to the arrest of this man and his cohorts.

Jack was not on his most-favored list.

Gus went on. "The word is he's just been released early for good behavior."

The fine hairs on Jack's neck bristled in warning. "Thanks for the info, Gus. But I've got work to do."

"I never forgot when you said, 'This story ain't over.' And you had the receipts to back it up."

Could this be related to the guy he'd overheard at the cafe? "It's been a long time, Gus."

"Not that long." The man paused. "Say, how's that cash flow going for you?"

Jack winced. That hurt. While the cost of living in Summer Beach was less than in New York, he had additional unexpected expenses pertaining to Leo. He wanted to provide a home for his son—and for Marina. When he'd rented this beach cottage, Bennett had negotiated a purchase option for him. Jack had been saving money to exercise the option and pay for some renovations. This was a major goal.

"Look, Jack. I've got a feeling you were right, so how about you pick up where you left off? You could get back in your groove with a timely story."

"I don't know…" Jack had to admit that it was tempting. An important story, maybe one that he could parlay into a major book deal, would be welcome.

They had a brief discussion about contract rights, and Gus was surprisingly generous. It was almost too good of a deal to pass up, but he still had to think about the impact this could have on Leo and Marina. He wouldn't put them in harm's way.

Maybe he could team up with a younger colleague, someone who didn't have a family to worry about. Like he'd once been. One that would take the risks.

"Are you still there, Jack?"

Jack scraped his stubbled chin. "I'll have to think about this. Can I let you know next week?"

"Next week is a long time. But I can do that for you. Let me hear from you." Gus hung up.

Jack stared at the screen. He knew the offer wouldn't be open long. Gus would move to the next story if Jack didn't grab the opportunity. That's just the way journalism was. The fact that Gus had thought to call him was surprising, too. Jack was usually the one making the story pitches. He couldn't help but think there was something more to this offer.

Was that related to the conversation he'd overheard?

Jack's mind shifted into overdrive. He'd have to consult his old notes and figure out the puzzle again. A thought seized him. No way would the old man make a direct threat. He'd always been more strategic, like a snake waiting for the right moment to strike for his vengeance.

Jack shivered at the thought. But he had found a new life in Summer Beach. Nothing would stop him from his job of caring for Leo and, if she would have him, spending his life with Marina.

Just then, Leo barreled from his room. "Hey, Dad. Who was at the door?"

"Just a delivery. Are you hungry yet?"

Leo put his hands on his stomach. "You gave me a giant turkey sandwich with potato chips and pickles this morning."

"And your point is?"

"I'm still stuffed. That wasn't breakfast."

"Sure it was. I used to eat pizza for breakfast."

"You still do, Dad."

He didn't realize Leo had noticed. One more bad habit to clean up. "I'll pick up eggs and cereal this afternoon."

"Can Samantha come over? Her mom can drop her off in a few minutes, and we can take Scout to the beach. Logan wants to go, too. And he asked if I can spend the night with him tonight."

"As long as it's okay with his parents." Logan was Bennett's nephew and lived in the house in back of theirs. Bennett's sister and her husband often asked Leo to supper.

"It is." Leo grabbed a beach towel from the bathroom.

"And stay away from the riptides."

"I've grown up at the beach, remember?"

That was true. Vanessa had owned a home in Santa Monica, so Leo probably knew more about the beach than he did.

Jack wrapped his son in a huge hug, lifting him off the floor. "It took me so long to find you, and I don't want to risk losing you now. Besides, your mom would kill me if you drowned while she was on her honeymoon. No way she wants to cut her trip to Europe short for that."

Leo grinned. "Love you, Dad."

"Love you, too, Leo." Jack ruffled his son's thick hair, which was so much like his own. "Go call Samantha." He paused, thinking about Gus and the conversation he'd heard at the cafe. "And I'm coming with you."

"We're okay on our own."

Jack feigned disappointment. "Hey, can't a dad tag along? I'll bring a cooler with juice boxes."

Leo made a face. "You know we're kind of old for those, right? But you can carry my sports bottle."

"Sure thing." Jack whistled for the dog. "Beach time, Scout."

The yellow Lab leapt to his feet, wagging his tail.

Jack chuckled to himself. He and Leo were doing just fine. What was wrong with pickles for breakfast anyway?

WHILE WATCHING LEO, Samantha, and Logan race back and forth with Scout on the beach, Jack made a call to his friend Bennett.

"What's up?"

"You sound like you're running."

"Just finished. It's that fundraiser at the school. Had to finish my laps."

"Oh yeah, I didn't realize that was today. Guess I owe you some money for that."

"You can write the big check to the school. They're collecting all the pledges."

"Will do. Hey, when you have time, I want to talk about buying this cottage. I have some savings. What do I need to do? I've never bought a home before." Besides being the town mayor, Bennet was also a real estate broker. He'd found the beach cottage for Jack.

"Come run with me tomorrow. We can talk about it then."

"Again? You'll do anything to get me on the beach at dawn."

Bennett chuckled. "Right you are."

Jack hung up and clasped his knees, watching Leo toss the ball to Scout. He was torn between his desire to provide for his son and the need to keep him safe. That went for Marina, too. But maybe he could bring in a researcher and co-writer. He'd dig through his contacts to see who he could find.

At least he could keep renting out the studio above the

garage. Surfers didn't care if the floor and walls were splattered with paint; it was like living in a Jackson Pollack painting. People thought it was cool and added to the ambiance.

The upstairs unit was nothing fancy. Jack had hauled up a couple of beds, along with a small refrigerator, coffee maker, and microwave. He moved a table and chairs onto the balcony. That was all most people needed, aside from good waves to ride.

He checked the time. The next group would be checking in later today. They were exhausting, changing their arrival date several times, and he'd had to hustle to get the rooms ready. He was so frustrated with their indecisiveness that he told them to call when they were getting close to Summer Beach.

With any luck, Jack could manage everything. He still owed Ginger's publisher some illustration changes for the next book in her series.

Between Leo's schedule and needs, cleaning up after the short-term tenants, juggling illustrations, and pitching future stories, Jack was aware that he was making a few mistakes, but this workload would soon pay off. He almost missed the days when he had one job to do and a single deadline.

Even with everything in his life, he'd never missed a due date. He'd come close the other day, but only because he forgot what day it was.

Shielding his eyes from the sun, he scanned the beach for anyone out of the ordinary, but it was only the usual tourists and kids on summer break. He gazed after Leo, Logan, and Samantha, who'd started racing each other, laughing as they stumbled and rolled in wet sand.

The kids and Scout would all need baths. Maybe he'd just hose them off in the backyard with their swimsuits on and toss them a bar of soap. Or get one of those pressure washer attachments. He chuckled at the fun they could have with that, although he might not tell Leo's mother about it.

Now he could empathize with overwhelmed parents. Maybe he could pitch a single father story about that, even though it wasn't exactly Pulitzer material. He'd write it under his new pen name, Jack Summers.

Still, the opportunity from Gus weighed on his mind. Jack would have to make a decision fast. If he wanted any part of his old career back—and the good money that came with it—this might be his last chance.

*a*fter their morning walk on the beach, Marina trailed Ginger through Java Beach, where neighbors greeted her grandmother like a celebrity. Even at her age, she still had an elegant bearing, her eyes sparkled with mischief, and her smile could light a room. Marina remembered her grandfather calling Ginger his secret diplomatic weapon. With her keen intelligence, charisma, and charm, she could disarm even the most taciturn guest, yet she didn't suffer fools or rude behavior. That was as true today as ever.

Ginger had standards, and they were as high as Mount Everest.

"Ms. Ginger, howdy do today?" An older man in a wrinkled Hawaiian shirt stood and tipped a battered straw hat. His cohorts at the table quickly shoved an assortment of folding bills aside as they acknowledged Ginger, too.

"Charlie, you wouldn't be tallying wagers this morning, would you? You know how Chief Clarkson frowns on that."

"No, ma'am, we're just settling the breakfast tab. Right, fellas?"

"Sure, sure," the men muttered in a chorus of uncertain agreement.

A woman with royal blue hair encircled with a sparkly rhinestone visor let out a chortle behind them. "Did Mitch raise his prices?" Darla asked. "Because breakfast never costs that much around here, Charlie."

Charlie pressed a finger to his lips and winked. "You didn't see anything, Darla."

"Two caramel macchiatos," the proprietor called out. Mitch stood behind a counter festooned with fishing nets and coconuts to resemble a Tiki bar. When Marina approached the counter, he said, "Good to see you. How's business?"

"Better now that I hired another cook." She'd hired Cruise to help her run the food truck and give her more flexibility. Cruise was more than a surfer bum—he'd worked in large hotel kitchens but had burned out. When she'd interviewed him, he'd told her that he wanted to have a more chill life in Summer Beach.

Marina picked up the whipped cream-topped coffees, licking the extra cream off her fingers as it spilled over the side. "This is delicious."

Mitch slid a few napkins across the counter for her. "You'll be glad to have help in the kitchen. That was one of the best moves I made here."

"I think it will be. Then I can relax for a couple of days during the week. And do things like catch up on the local gossip here."

"Always plenty of that. Lately, everyone has been wondering when the wedding is going to be. Kai's, I mean." Mitch gave her a sheepish grin.

Marina ignored the implied reference to herself.

"Guess they can't wait." He swiped the counter with a rag and smiled. "I know how that is. When it's right, why wait?"

Without expecting an answer to that, Mitch raised his hand to the next people in line, and Marina moved on.

Soon, she and Jack might be the topic of conversation at Java Beach. Holding the coffees aloft, Marina cut through the crowd. Half the people were dressed in shorts and swimsuit coverups for the beach, while the locals were nearly as casually attired. Many, like Arthur from Antique Times and George from the hardware store next door, would spill out to their shops soon, and Summer Beach would be open for business.

Marina and Ginger selected a table beneath a vintage travel poster advertising the South Pacific, and nearby patrons made room for them in the small space. The tables were so close it was almost impossible to have a private conversation here. Fortunately, the table behind them was leaving.

Marina waggled her fingers in a wave at Louise, a sturdy, steel-haired woman who ran the village laundry and dry cleaners. She often ordered the spinach salad at the Coral Cafe.

Ginger turned to Arthur. "Anything interesting come into the shop lately?"

Arthur ran a hand over his smoothly shaven head. "A square Lalique bowl with a rose pattern," he replied in his English accent. "Very fine quality. One of your granddaughters might fancy that. And I just received a pair of Gorham candlesticks once used at Las Brisas del Mar on consignment. Sterling silver with interesting mixed metals, more than a hundred years old. Fine art pieces, in my opinion."

Ginger raised her brow in alarm. "Oh, dear. Is Ivy selling pieces from the inn?"

Heads swiveled their way, and Marina touched Ginger's hand in warning. Though Ivy had her challenges converting the old house to an inn, Marina didn't want people to think her friend's business was in trouble—especially Darla, who was Ivy's neighbor. She was the town's busybody, yet she had a soft spot for Mitch and regarded him as a son.

Arthur shook his head. "These date from before Ivy took over the old beach house. Amelia Erickson gave them to one of her friends, as I understand. The woman's son consigned the candlesticks. They'd make a fine wedding gift."

"I'll stop by." Ginger pressed a hand to her chest. "Not for myself, of course, but for someone who would appreciate them."

Arthur grinned. "Would that be Kai or Marina?"

Again, the conversation level dimmed, and Marina felt her chest flush. Sipping her macchiato, she braced herself.

In a loud whisper, Darla asked, "Have you and Jack set a date?"

Ginger cleared her throat. "Darla, I promise you'll be among the first to know if Marina deems Jack worthy of her many attributes."

At that, Marina nearly choked on her coffee. Ginger was always quick to come to her defense.

The women at Darla's table began speaking about Jack among themselves, and Marina wished she could melt through the floor. Instead, she put a tight smile on her face. "I can hear you all. I'm sitting right here, ladies."

One of the women leaned forward. "We want to know if you and Jack are still seriously dating. Because if you're not, my niece would—ouch!" She glared at Darla and leaned down to rub her shin. "Why did you do that?"

"Because you're making a darn fool of yourself," Darla replied. "Let's go and leave these two in peace." She mouthed the word *sorry* to Marina.

Darla might be abrasive, but beneath her rough exterior, she cared about people. She must have realized her question made Marina uncomfortable.

After the table of women left, Ginger leaned forward. "That was a little awkward."

Marina caught her meaning. "Not my fault."

"No, indeed." Ginger inclined her head and tapped her chin in thought. "I met with Jack last week about illustrations for the book." She hesitated. "Have you noticed any change in Jack's behavior lately?"

"He can be preoccupied, or maybe he's nervous about you

know what." Marina could read Ginger. "Or he's still adjusting to having Leo. A boy that age can be very active." Leo was a curious, inquisitive youngster, probably much as Jack had been. "I wonder what Leo will think about..."

Ginger reached for her hand and squeezed it. "You'll tell me all about it tomorrow."

"Of course."

Ginger gave a satisfied nod. With that seemingly settled, she went on. "Has Kai shared her wedding plans with you?"

"Not much, other than she wants to move it up."

"And did she tell you why?"

The obvious thought struck Marina. "No, but they're clearly committed to one another."

"Thank heavens for that." Ginger gave her a pointed look.

"Regardless of the situation, we should help Kai have the wedding she's always dreamed of. I've offered, but she's been very secretive about their plans. Except for needing a dress right away."

"Kai is certainly moving quickly."

"Her friends are in between shows. Maybe that had something to do with it, too."

"Perhaps that's the reason for the rush." Yet Ginger's doubtful expression belied her words. A moment later, her eyes brightened. "I have some items I know you'll both want to look at. Every bride needs something old. And something new."

"I'll be sure to tell Kai."

They chatted a little more before returning to the cottage, making their way through the village this time. Shops were opening, and throngs of tourists were already out in shorts and flip-flops. High season in Summer Beach meant lively crowds all summer, eager to spend money and make memories. After working hard all season, some shopkeepers closed for a month or more in the winter, taking their holidays.

As they approached a boutique, Ginger slowed. "Do you have anything to wear to Kai's wedding?"

"I have no idea where it will be. Knowing Kai, it could be on a boat."

Ginger paused and nodded toward a window display of a chic, black linen dress paired with sunny yellow and white accents. "That dress would be stunning on you."

"For the wedding?" Marina raised her brow. "But it's black."

Ginger shook her head. "For your date with Jack tonight. You should try it on."

Marina hesitated. She loved the scooped neckline, and it looked like it would flatter her silhouette and flare around her calves. "I've already put out a dress to wear. I don't really need it."

"Maybe not, but you certainly deserve it. Let's go in. My treat," she added.

Ginger led the way into the boutique, where an array of sundresses were artfully paired with sandals and accessories. Mango-scented candles filled the shop with their sweet scent, instantly lifting Marina's spirits.

By the time they emerged, Marina had the lovely black linen dress in a bag looped over her arm, along with a pair of strappy, high-heeled sandals. Her grandmother had promised to lend her a strand of silvery-gray South Sea pearls and earrings that Marina adored.

"That ensemble looks fabulous on you," Ginger said. "Like something Audrey Hepburn might have worn."

Marina laughed. "I'm not sure how far I can walk in these shoes until I break them in."

Arching an eyebrow, Ginger asked, "Isn't Jack picking you up tonight?"

"He asked me to meet him there." Marina didn't know why, but she assumed it had something to do with his plans. "I'm sure he'll bring me home."

"I would certainly hope so. I have to go out later, so I can drop you off at Beaches."

Marina quickly agreed. "And I love this new outfit, but you didn't have to buy it for me."

"Nonsense. A woman needs to feel pampered from time to time. You do so much for others. Besides, I have a good feeling about tonight."

Marina sighed at the thought. With Kai's wedding plans shifting into high gear, the longing Marina felt for Jack filled her thoughts more often.

Ginger paused and peered at Marina's hair.

"What's wrong?"

"Your hair has become so long. It's lovely, but why don't you call that new salon and see if they could fit you in today?"

"You mean Beach Waves?"

"That's the one. I've heard the owner is a magician with hair. And don't worry about the cost. Ask for a relaxed, modern cut, not like those ultra-sleek lacquered styles you used to wear on the news program. Maybe a fresh color, too. Surprise Jack with a new look. My Bertrand always enjoyed that."

Marina had been wearing her hair up in a clip while she worked in the kitchen. As a news anchor, she'd once had to spend a fortune on her hair, but since moving to Summer Beach, she'd ditched the straightened locks, red nails, and stiletto heels that had been her on-camera uniform. It had felt good to do that, but she had to admit she wasn't as polished as she used to be. Natural didn't mean sloppy.

Suddenly excited at the prospect, Marina hugged her grandmother. "I'll see if I can get in this afternoon."

LATER THAT DAY, Marina eased into a chair in front of a large mirror at the new, artsy salon in the village. Pink divans popped against aquamarine walls, which showcased photos of women with flowing locks of various styles.

She leaned in, inspecting the lighter strands in her brown hair. Most were sun-bleached, but a few around her face were undeniably white. She frowned at the daring interlopers.

"Not today, you don't." She yanked one out. How long could she keep doing that?

The owner of the shop walked up behind her and touched her hand. "Hold up. I can take care of those if you want. But silver is a hot trend. What would you like today?"

"I'd like a natural, beachy look," Marina said, raising her gaze and eyeing different styles. "But I'm not sure what I mean by that." She pointed to a poster of a lean woman with a mane of hair. "How about that look? And the body to go along with it."

Brandy smiled and shook her head. "You're beautiful just as you are, but I can give your hair some highlights and shine that will bring out your eyes and complement your skin tone. That one you like is a technique called Balayage. Essentially, it means to sweep or paint light-kissed accents throughout your hair." Circling the chair, Brandy inspected Marina's hair. "That style is subtle but sexy. It would look fabulous on you."

"That's exactly what I need." Excitement fluttered through her. "Let's do this."

Marina was confident that she was in the talented hands of an artist. The younger woman, whose own hair shimmered like golden cognac with a masterfully shaded ombre look, was the proprietor of Beach Waves, a new salon that specialized in trendy beach hair. Her hands bore an intricate henna design, and she wore washed silk palazzos with beaded slippers and a tank top.

Brandy had told her that she had recently moved from Malibu, trading the glitz of the celebrity beach colony for the slower pace of Summer Beach.

Closing her eyes as Brandy worked, Marina imagined how

pleased Jack would be when he saw her. She could hardly wait to surprise him with her new look. Ginger's comment floated into her mind.

It wasn't often that Marina took the time to pamper herself, so she relaxed into the experience, enjoying every moment. She had a feeling that tonight would be a pivotal point in their relationship. She could feel it all the way to her toes, which she wriggled in delight. Her future stretched ahead of her.

Tonight would be a night to remember.

6

*L*ater that evening, Marina strolled into Beaches, feeling confident in the new black linen sundress that fit her perfectly. She ran a hand along the smooth fabric that skimmed her hips. Even if she didn't have a bikini body anymore, this dress hid her imperfections and made her look like a million dollars. She could say that with confidence because Ginger had approved it, and she never lied. Except when her grandmother embellished old stories. But that was allowed under dramatic license, Ginger would claim.

Marina caught a glimpse of her profile in a mirror. Gone, too, was her sun-frazzled hair. Brandy had sprinkled golden-auburn accents throughout her natural brown hair, bestowing a second helping of confidence upon her.

She lifted her chin and touched Ginger's silvery-gray South Sea pearls nestled at her neck. She'd even touched her wrists with her finest perfume.

Tonight was her night. For once, everything was going her way.

When the maître d' greeted her at the entry, Russell's eyebrows arched, and he stepped back to admire her updated appearance.

"Oh-la-la! You've been hiding all this fabulousness under your chef jacket and sensible shoes."

Marina laughed and dropped a little curtsey in her high heels. "Think Jack will like it?"

"If he doesn't, you'll have no trouble finding a replacement."

Russell often visited the Coral Cafe for lunch on his days off from Beaches. They'd become friends after the Scout catastrophe at the restaurant. Jack had worked to get back on Russell's good side.

If Marina felt a sliver of self-consciousness over her new look, Russell quickly dispelled the feeling with an approving smile. Not that she needed his validation, but it was fun to be admired as if she were twenty again.

Russell tapped his reservation book. "I saw Jack's request on the list, so I've held the best table for you. The sunset should be magnificent tonight." He glanced at his watch. "Perfect timing, too."

He gestured toward a table near a plate-glass window where waves crashed against rocks outside, sending up sprays of misty crescendos. "Would you like to sit down now?"

"I'll wait for Jack."

"Have a seat at the bar then. We have some interesting guests you can talk to."

Russell led the way. As Marina passed, she nodded at a few people she knew. One man, in particular, looked familiar, but she couldn't place him. From the double-takes and smiles, she knew she was making an impression.

Russell stopped by a polished wooden bar. A pianist played nearby, and ornate bottles gleamed in the low lights.

"We've just opened a new bottle of champagne—a very fine one. I'll tell Chef Marguerite you've arrived."

"That sounds wonderful, thanks. I've been dying for her food ever since the Taste of Summer Beach cook-off last year."

"We gained a lot of new customers from that event. Are you planning another one?"

"Next year. It was a lot of work, and with the opening of the cafe and the summer rush, I've been slammed."

Not to mention the new food truck. It had passed inspection, and she had wired Judith a deposit through her bank. She would have it painted when she had time, as that process would take a few days. That meant the new look wouldn't be ready for Kai's opening night at the Seashell, but she'd figure out how to make it work. All she needed to do was cover the submarine illustration and logo.

The amphitheater would provide a good trial run, as customers could collect their preordered picnic boxes there. Marina had a simple menu already planned, and she could hardly wait.

"Glad your place is doing well." Russell pulled out a chair at the bar for her. "With the high tide, you'll see some spectacular waves tonight." He gestured toward the bartender. "Chef Marguerite's special reserve champagne for Chef Marina."

She thanked Russell before he made his way to the front to greet another couple who'd just arrived.

While she watched, the bartender slowly poured a glass for her. As she raised the glass, pale golden bubbles tickled her lips. Sipping, she watched the sun sink toward the purple horizon as waves crashed intermittently against an outcropping of rocks. This was the most dramatic dining view in Summer Beach.

Jack should be here any minute.

She glanced around the restaurant. The sunset was already bathing the dining area in a rosy glow. Shell-pink tablecloths and a profusion of coral and pink flowers graced every table. Casual, well-dressed couples lingered over bottles of wine and some of the best cuisine in Summer Beach. From a nearby table, crystal chimed as a couple toasted one another. Exquisite aromas wafted from the kitchen.

This was Marina's version of heaven. She swept her hair across her bare shoulder and cradled her chin in her hand. As the minutes ticked, she sat enjoying the privilege of being a guest tonight, watching the servers carry Chef Marguerite's artistically rendered dishes to delighted diners.

A few minutes later, a stout woman in a white chef jacket bustled out. Her hair was swept back, and she wore the same sturdy shoes Marina wore in her kitchen.

"I'm glad you're joining us tonight," Chef Marguerite said. "And I love your hair. Did you have that done in town?"

"Brandy at Beach Waves did it."

"If I ever get out of the kitchen, I'll have to see her." The two women laughed, and Marguerite added, "You look like you're ready for a very special occasion."

"Anytime you're cooking for me is special," Marina replied, sidestepping the question. "I've been dreaming of your shrimp Provençal for months."

Marguerite chuckled. "And I've been drooling over your seafood pizza that won the Taste of Summer Beach."

They talked for a short while, comparing dishes they'd had at other restaurants that they'd enjoyed. Marguerite mentioned how much she'd enjoyed Kai's shows at the Seashell theater, and Marina shared that Kai and Axe had moved up the wedding. She didn't know how Kai was going to manage the new summer show she and Axe had planned.

"They make a great couple. Happy to have you all at Beaches for a rehearsal dinner."

"Kai is still making plans, but we'll keep that in mind. This would be a lovely venue for the family."

"And a professional discount for you, of course." Marguerite excused herself to return to the kitchen.

Sipping her champagne, Marina chatted with the bartender and other patrons at the bar. The attractive man who looked oddly familiar seemed interested in her, and although she didn't encourage him, she was flattered by his attention.

Finally, he leaned his tall frame over the stool that separated them. "I'm Jay, and I've just moved to Summer Beach. I've heard this is one of the best restaurants in town."

Marina couldn't resist. "Along with the Coral Cafe."

He snapped his fingers. "That's the other one people have been telling me about."

With a trim physique and a sprinkling of gray in his glossy black hair, Jay seemed about Marina's age. They chatted for a few minutes, and she asked what brought him to Summer Beach.

"I'm a pediatrician," Jay replied. "I'm acquiring a small practice here. Do you know Dr. Singh?"

Marina nodded. Now she remembered. Gilda had pointed him out at the Seabreeze Inn during Vanessa's wedding. "Everyone around here knows her as Dr. Dede. She often comes to my restaurant for lunch—that's the Coral Cafe. I heard she was retiring soon, so you must be the new guy."

"That I am." Jay chuckled.

"And is she really your aunt?"

He nodded. "I guess word travels fast here."

"Especially if you're a good-looking single doctor." As soon as the words left her mouth, Marina wished she could take them back.

Jay tilted his head back and laughed. "Well, I'll admit to two out of three."

"Oh, I'm sorry." Marina's face grew warm. "I'd heard you weren't married."

His deep, dark eyes twinkled. "They got that part right."

And modest, too, she thought. He asked about her cafe and seemed genuinely interested, asking questions about how she'd started it and what her most popular dishes were. "I hope you'll visit. It's close to the village and your office."

"I'll be sure to stop by as soon as I can."

As they chatted, the sun slipped beneath the horizon, and Marina felt as if her heart were doing the same. She kept glancing at the door. During a lull in the conversation, she checked the time.

Jack had missed the spectacular sunset he'd planned for. She prayed nothing had happened to him or Leo.

Russell approached Jay and his friends. "Your table is ready," he announced.

"It's been a real pleasure speaking with you," Jay said, lingering behind the others. "Are you sure your friend is coming? Because if not, you're welcome to join us."

"Thank you, but I'm sure he'll be here soon."

He hesitated. "I hope I'm not being too forward, but you look lovely tonight. And it's been a real pleasure talking to you."

Marina tilted her head and thanked him. A warm glow gathered in her chest. Jay was a nice addition to Summer Beach.

She waited at the bar, nursing her glass of champagne as she sent a text to Jack. Something must have delayed him. He didn't answer, but maybe he was driving. Jack often ran late. Still, he could be here any minute, she told herself.

A woman on the other side of her struck up a conversation, which helped pass the time. She noticed that Jay's table was served, but there was still no sign of Jack.

Her worry escalated. Something was definitely wrong.

When the other woman and her husband left to be seated, Marina took her phone from her purse again and tapped another message.

I'm here.

She waited.

This time, he replied. *I don't see you.*

She turned around, looking for him. *At the bar.*

He replied: *?????*

She wasn't getting anywhere with texts. With a sigh, she tapped his number. "Hi, honey."

"The door is open. Just come in." Jack sounded rushed.

"No. I'm at—"

"Okay, look, I can't talk right now. Call you later?"

"What? Jack, I'm—"

"Sorry, really can't talk. I'll explain later."

Click.

Marina stared at the phone, dumbfounded. What was that all about? Maybe something had happened to Leo. Her heart raced with worry.

She tapped his number again.

"What?" he said sharply.

"Is Leo hurt?" She rushed out the words before he could hang up again.

"What? I'm sure he's fine. He's spending the night at Logan's house. Look—"

"Are *you* okay?"

"Yeah, yeah," he said, brushing off her concern.

"Then what?"

"Can't talk. Gotta go."

"I'm at Beaches!" She hurled out the words. This was confounding—and not at all like Jack.

Jack let out a curse. "What day is it?"

"You know what day it is. I'll wait." She blew out a breath of exasperation. "They're holding a table for us, but not for much longer."

"No, I can't. Not tonight. I'm sorry. Just have dinner without me." He paused. "Look, we have to talk."

"You're right about that." Seething now, Marina hung up.

She blinked back hot tears that sprang to her eyes and guided her glass to lips trembling with anger, worry, and disappointment. What was going on with him?

She motioned to Russell, who quickly strode toward her.

He had already checked in with her a couple of times. She knew she was holding up their reservations queue.

"I just talked to Jack." Marina shook her head, barely able to speak. "He's not coming."

Russell's expression fell. "I hope he's alright."

"He's being…I don't know, just Jack," she spat out, embarrassed at the situation.

"I'm so sorry for you. Another time?"

Marina nodded mutely. She'd been sipping champagne, pleased with her new look and anticipating their conversation tonight. And now this. How dare he tell her to have dinner by herself?

A pivotal evening. Indeed it was. A hot wave of anger surged through her. How could he have forgotten? They had talked about tonight several times. He was making up for the disaster Scout had caused, not that it was the dog's fault. That had been all Jack's.

Feeding hot sauce on a taco to a dog? With an inflamed mouth, Scout had charged for her at the restaurant after he'd seen her go in with Cole. She squeezed her eyes shut, remembering the way poor Scout had sought shelter—and a lot of water and hugs—from her.

Now, once again, Jack had ruined what should have been a beautiful evening. And maybe the rest of their lives.

Worse, it sounded like he was wrapped up in some story— she recognized that distracted sound in his voice from her years in a newsroom. But what could possibly have been more important? It didn't matter. Whatever it was, it was more important to him than she was. He lived mere minutes away. He still could have changed and joined her. She bit her lip to hold back her tears.

Just then, Jay's deep voice washed over her. "I know we've just met, but is there anything I can do for you? It looks like you've just received some unfortunate news."

Marina wished she could disappear. "I need to leave. My...boyfriend—" She stopped. What exactly was he now?

She fumbled with her purse, letting her hair fall over her face to cover her shame. Had she been expecting too much of Jack tonight? Kai must have been wrong about what she'd seen. Clearly, because the man just couldn't deliver.

Jay was staring at her with magnificent dark eyes that seemed steeped in kindness. This was a man devoted to caring for children.

"If you need a ride home, I can take you."

Marina shook her head and eased off the stool. "You're having dinner. And I live just down the beach."

He frowned. "Is it far?"

"It's a short walk." She pushed her hair aside and forced a smile at his thoughtfulness. "I'll be okay. I'm just upset about my date."

"Big mistake on his part." Jay's gaze traveled down to her feet. "You shouldn't have to walk in those lovely shoes. My car is just outside. I promise I'll deliver you safely."

When she hesitated, he added, "Relax, I'm mom-approved."

Marina smiled through her anguish. "Do you know how corny that sounds?"

"Guess it's good that my stint as a stand-up comic in college didn't work out."

A hero with a sense of humor. She managed a wan smile.

As Jay waved goodbye to his friends and held the door for her, she could feel all eyes on them. This news would certainly travel around town. *Serves Jack right,* she thought, setting her jaw against another wave of angry disappointment.

How could Jack have done this to her—and with such a flimsy explanation?

7

"*H*old up a minute," Jack called to Bennett as he paused on the sand, resting his hands on his bare knees. A moment later, Jack dropped to one knee, suddenly overcome with something he couldn't pinpoint. The bright morning sun burned his eyes, and his chest felt like it was being tightened in a vise grip.

Maybe because he wasn't used to running two days in a row, but he'd needed to do something this morning. Last night after Marina called, he'd downed a few tequila shots, angry at himself for letting this situation get to him.

He wouldn't have forgotten their date otherwise. It had meant everything to him, and he'd been kicking himself for it. He'd thought it was the next day. Once again he'd forgotten what day it was.

Bennett slowed to a trot and turned around. "Hey, you're not looking so good. Need some help, bud?" He started back toward him.

Jack held up a hand. "I don't think I can manage the rest of this run."

Honestly, all he wanted was a cigarette. Even though it

had been more than a year since he'd quit, his stress level had blasted off the chart.

Bennett stood near him, his hands on his hips. "Were you feeling sick this morning?"

"I don't think I'm ill. Just out of shape."

"You've been increasing your time and looking pretty good." Bennett hesitated. "Got something on your mind?"

"Always," Jack allowed, though he didn't elaborate.

He wasn't one to confide in many people, though Bennett was pretty close friends with Mitch and a few others around the village. He made a good mayor because he actually cared about the quality of life for people in Summer Beach.

After investigating egregious wrong-doings for years, Jack had seen the gamut of human feelings, from those who couldn't care less about their fellow man, to others who cared too much for their own good. Bennett seemed to occupy the balanced middle ground. All Jack could do was trust his gut, which usually served him well.

Bennett knelt beside him as if he was concerned Jack might keel over. "Is it Leo?"

Jack could have gone for the obvious, but he shook his head. "He's a great kid."

"Then, is this about Marina?"

"I'm lucky to have her, too." Jack pushed a hand through his hair, damp with morning dew. If she'd still have him.

Bennett glanced around. They were alone, but he still lowered his voice. "Having second thoughts?"

"Not about Marina. Though I can't speak for her clearly lacking sense of discernment. She could have anyone."

Last holiday season, an old friend of her husband's had visited. *Cole.* The guy was a Marine, and Jack had a hard time keeping up with him. Sure, he had been concerned. Jealous, even. And he imagined there were plenty more where that one came from.

"You've got a lot going on." Bennett stretched out a leg as

he spoke. "Stepping up to care for Leo has taken some adjusting, I imagine. I thought I was going to have my own child once. That was pretty sobering."

"Leo is the best thing that's ever happened to me." Jack knew Bennett had lost his wife and unborn child to a rare condition she'd had during her pregnancy. Maybe that's why he was so compassionate.

Bennett was staring at him with such an empathetic expression—rare among his often jaded, seen-it-all friends from his profession. Jack rubbed his temples. "I have what you might call a professional conflict."

Bennett eased back on his heels. "Want to talk about it?"

"Afraid it's confidential." A year off, and he was getting soft. "I should head back to the house."

Bennett stood and gave Jack a hand up. "Get some rest. I'll check on those mortgage terms you asked about."

Before Bennett could say anything else, Jack drew a measured breath to make sure he wasn't dying before trotting home.

Although he might prefer that to facing Marina. He needed to call her today. And he had to make up for last night. Somehow.

The cottage was half a block from the beach, but it seemed like forever as he jogged toward it. On second thought, would Marina be happy there?

She'd lived in a nice apartment in San Francisco, and her grandmother's cottage was spacious and immaculately maintained. Although small by most standards, his house was a palace compared to the shoebox-sized apartments he'd rented in New York over the years.

When Jack was on extended or back-to-back assignments, he often dropped off what little he owned at a friend's home on Long Island. The old VW van he'd bought to drive to California had fit his needs. In a nod to Cervantes and Steinbeck, he'd named it *Rocinante*. He might still be living in that if not for Leo.

Most likely, he'd be back in New York chasing another story. And he never would have met Marina.

Arriving at his cottage, Jack stepped inside. The clapboard house had belonged to an artist, and murals of beach scenes were splashed across the walls. Some might call it a funky beach style, but he appreciated the art. Four white walls would have driven him crazy.

Being here in Summer Beach was enough of a challenge, even though he loved being part of the community. It reminded him of the small town he'd grown up in—only with a beach and great sunsets.

The sunset. He chastised himself again. How could he have forgotten?

He knew the answer. His life was out of control.

Jack popped a coffee pod into a machine, started a fresh brew, and waited, chewing the side of his mouth instead of reaching for the emergency cigarettes he'd hidden. Despite that, his gaze trailed toward an upper cabinet. Inside, his contraband was hidden behind an unused crock-pot Leo's mother had given him.

Chewing a new section of his lip, he resisted. Those mints he was practically addicted to didn't go well with coffee.

As soon as the coffee maker gurgled to a stop, he grabbed his cup and made his way to the work area he'd created in the sunroom of his bedroom. A half-drawn illustration for Ginger's upcoming children's book lay on the desk. That hardly seemed like work to him—drawing had been a hobby for years. He still hoped to get Ginger's story out of her some-day, but that wouldn't happen until she was ready.

Ginger Delavie. Ace code-breaker, mathematician, diplomat's widowed wife, and friend to many in high places. No telling what secrets Ginger was hiding. Probably many she'd take to her grave, though he hoped that wouldn't be for a long, long time. She was still sharper than most people far younger. Someday she might let him write her story—if he could cram it into his schedule.

If he and Marina got together, what would that make Ginger to him? His grandmother-in-law?

Good enough, he decided as he stared at the illustration of three little girls. Ginger's stories were based on tales she'd once told her granddaughters, Marina, Kai, and Brooke. They were all characters in the adventures.

This was his life now, and he had to find a way to make it pay. Ginger's books were just being published now. While the advances had been good, he discovered he couldn't live on that alone.

He couldn't take Leo from Summer Beach to a high-rise in New York, though many did. He didn't find fault with them, but Jack had grown up on a farm, and roaming through nature had kept him grounded. That's what he wanted for Leo. Even if he had to juggle a variety of odd jobs to do it.

In the corner, a sturdy battery-powered clock ticked in the silence, mocking him while he wondered if it was too early to call Marina.

He dreaded this call, but the longer he put it off, the bigger the rat he'd feel like.

As Jack was contemplating the drawing—one child could use a more surprised expression, and he decided to add the dog in the scene—his phone buzzed with a message on a secure app he used with other journalists.

Can u talk?

It was Dane, one of his former colleagues from New York following up on Jack's call from last night—the one he'd been talking to when Marina called. After talking with his editor, Gus, Jack had reached out to Dane to get updated intel about the man who had just been released from prison.

Jack rolled his shoulders. *Here we go again.* Long ago, he'd hoped this would go away. Heaving a sigh, he tapped back.

Sure. Years ago, Dane assisted Jack with research for that explosive story. If anyone could track down information, it was him. Jack needed to connect the dots to see if he was in danger in Summer Beach.

He took a swig of coffee before the phone rang. "Hey. What's up?"

"It's about your guy." Dane had scant details. "Are you covering this again?"

Jack couldn't do this to Leo or Marina. "I'm out of this, man. I've decided."

"You're never out. Not after…you know, what happened."

Jack paced the line of windows, watching storm clouds gathering over the ocean. The memory of the conversation he had heard at the cafe haunted him, and his chest tightened again. "Let's say he knows where I am now. How'd he find out?"

A thought occurred to him. Dane could be baiting him. Jack could imagine the headlines. *Mob Boss Exacts Revenge on Journalist.* Torn between disbelief and anger, he blurted out a few choice words. "Was it you? I'm not going to be part of your story."

"Wasn't me, dude. Give me some credit. Wouldn't be helping you now if it was."

"Why, then?"

"I still owe you one."

Jack nodded at that. "At least."

A strained laugh followed, and Jack blew out a breath. "Is that all?"

"I'll keep you updated. Watch your back."

"Always." Jack tapped off the call. That wasn't necessarily true; he'd grown a little complacent since landing in Summer Beach.

Covering wars meant keeping out of the line of fire, but the investigative work he'd done had farther-reaching, more sinister implications. What he'd unearthed had brought down illegal empires and imprisoned people. And worse. But he wasn't the one to blame. *Do the crime, you do the time—however you interpret that.*

Feeling suddenly vulnerable, Jack shot a look around the sunroom. Wide windows let in plenty of sunlight.

And left him exposed.

Yet, recalling what he knew of the guy, he wouldn't be so obvious. Still, Jack packed his work and moved to the kitchen table, drawing the cheery yellow curtains. On second thought, he swung open the back door and whistled for Scout. Fortunately, Leo was still at Logan's home.

Waiting for Scout, he wondered how he could bring Marina into such a situation? And this might not be the only time.

Frowning, Jack peered out the door. Where was Scout? He usually came right away. Worried, Jack glanced around the small yard shaded with fruit trees and whistled again. "Hey, boy. Where are you? Get over here."

This time, Scout bounded toward him with his lopsided gait, and Jack let out a breath of relief. He shooed him inside and rewarded him with a treat. Still an overgrown puppy, Scout plopped beside the table.

"New routine, new duty. Now you're a guard dog, got it?" Settling down to work, Jack eyed the high kitchen cabinet, still bent on resisting, though his resolve was being tested today.

Not yet, he told himself. With any luck, not ever again. He unwrapped a new tin of mints to use as a coffee chaser and turned his attention back to his work.

It was still too early to call Marina.

As he sketched the dog in the drawing, he jiggled his leg under the table, worried more for Leo and Marina than himself.

Just then, Scout picked up his head and barked at a window.

With his heart hammering, Jack spun around. Through the slit in the curtains, he spied a bird teasing Scout.

Jack got up and fished a dog treat from a box on the counter. "Good boy, just keep an eye out for bigger prey, would you?" He gave Scout another treat as a reward, and the dog crunched happily by Jack's feet, sending crumbs scattering.

As he closed the gap in the curtains, Jack wondered how he was going to tell Marina about this, especially after last night. He'd had the evening planned, but between his irresponsible short-term guests switching dates and the worry he had about this man being released from prison, he'd lost track of the days.

He'd honestly thought their dinner was tonight. Why didn't she say something to him on the beach yesterday morning?

Silently, he chastised himself. He couldn't blame this disaster on her. Or anyone else, for that matter. No, he'd made this mess

As he watched the minutes tick by before calling Marina, he thought about the offer his editor had made to him. There was still an unfinished element to the story, though Jack knew it might cost him dearly to complete it.

For now, he thought that chapter should be someone else's to write. Jack heaved a sigh over the lost opportunity, but he could no longer risk that investigative story.

With any luck, this situation would blow over soon. In the meantime, it would definitely change his plans with Marina. She'd already been widowed once, and he wouldn't impose that on her again. Or, for that matter, his son.

Jack stared at his phone. If Dane confirmed what he suspected, he could take his van and get lost in the mountains until this blew over, though he had never been one to back down before. This was his life, and he was determined to stay in Summer Beach with Leo. But he didn't want to lead anyone to his son or Marina.

Then he remembered how long Vanessa would be on her honeymoon. He put his pencil down and drew his hands over his eyes. What on earth was he going to do with Leo?

8

*I*n Marina's dream, her phone rang, and it was Jack, laughing at her naiveté. She pulled a pillow over her head to shut out the nightmare.

All night she'd tossed in her lonely bed, angry yet still worried about what happened to him. Stupidly, perhaps. Most of all, she was upset with herself for letting yet another man get to her. First, Grady in San Francisco, and now, Jack.

How could she have been so blinded by his charm, his intelligence…and Leo and Scout? That needy trio was like catnip to middle-aged women, and that's what she was, no matter how good her hair looked or how many new dresses she wore.

Could Jack be just another Grady—the man she'd been engaged to who'd publicly dumped her for a younger model? That had destroyed her career, too. She had her conniving younger colleague to thank for that on-air bombshell, but it was Marina's fault that she'd gotten involved with such a creep.

Just then, her phone buzzed—this time, it was for real—jolting her from her distressing dream. She flopped over, peering at the small screen on the nightstand.

A photo flashed on the screen.

Jack. That was no dream she'd had.

She grappled for her phone, but it slid onto the floor, bouncing off the braided rug and onto the hardwood floor, where it continued its annoyingly chirpy ring. As she scrambled for it, her leg became entangled in the sheet. Reaching for the phone, she tumbled out of bed and landed with a thud on her hip.

In the bedroom next to Marina's, Kai banged on the wall. "Answer it, will you?"

Cursing under her breath, Marina grabbed the unrelenting device. "What?"

"Did I wake you?"

"What do you think, Einstein?"

Before she could ask what had happened to him last night —not that she cared to hear about it now—he launched into a litany of excuses.

"It's been a bit wild lately."

"Oh, really?" After tapping the speaker button, Marina kicked her way out of the tangled sheet that had slid off with her and leaned against the old iron bed in her thin cotton nightgown. This was going to take some time, and she hadn't even had a cup of coffee yet.

"I had Leo, you know." Jack went on about how he'd been occupied with his son all weekend.

"Just like a lot of others. Welcome to parenthood."

Jack paused, probably reaching for another excuse from his suitcase of defenses.

"And I've been so busy with Ginger's illustrations. When I sit down, hours just fly by."

"Uh-huh." That was number two. Were there more? She winced and rubbed her hip, which was throbbing with pain.

"Then, I had a friend who really needed to talk."

Number three. Now we're getting somewhere, Marina thought. "Was this friend in imminent physical danger?"

"You don't understand."

"I'm trying, but it sounds like you simply forgot."

"I swear it wasn't like that."

"Jack," she said, drawing out his name like a warning. "Either you did, or you didn't." Now she was sounding like the no-nonsense Ginger she'd grown up with.

"Something came up. An old friend threw me off my game."

"I suppose this friend is more important than the plans we'd made?"

Another pause. "It's hard to explain."

"Maybe you should start with this: Is your friend a man or a woman?"

"Why would that matter?"

"Surely you don't mean that." Marina glanced at the time. She was wide awake now with a big day ahead. And she was wasting her time here. "I don't want to argue. We need to decide what we're going to do next. If not, I have more important things to do."

"Can we plan a do-over tonight?"

Marina pushed her hair from her face. She was livid that he would confess that some old friend had usurped his time and act like it was no big deal. And try to make a date for tonight when he should remember they were having a beach barbecue for Kai and Axe.

She was not going to explain that to him. He could search for that in his tiny memory bank all by himself. She was tired of being taken for granted.

"Jack, I can't."

She tapped off the phone. Is this how it would end?

Drawing her hands over her face, she tried to put last night into perspective. What if it hadn't been such an important night? The night he was going to propose to her?

And then with a start, she thought, what if she'd conjectured that scenario, and it had been all in her mind? She couldn't blame it on Kai, either. Her sister saw what she saw. Maybe it *was* just dinner to him.

Not a proposal.

Maybe she'd latched onto a fantasy in her overactive monkey brain.

But he'd still stood her up.

And maybe he'd honestly forgotten. Was that worth destroying their relationship over?

Groaning, Marina pushed herself from the floor. She scooped up the sheet and threw it onto the bed in a clump. She couldn't think about this anymore.

She stuffed her arms into a robe, wondering if Jack would remember what they had planned this evening.

Though her heart was crushed, her logical side told her to give him one more chance for tonight. In a very tiny voice, that is.

That way, if Jack disappointed her again, she would know that he wasn't ready for a commitment, no matter what buttery smooth words he might try on her.

This approach made sense to her.

Marina turned off the ringer on her phone and tossed it onto the bed. It was time to get on with her life. She set her jaw, determined to shift her focus to her family and business.

She had plenty to occupy her time. Kai's friends and party plans. Her new food truck. The Seashell opening.

Living some romantic fantasy about a hot single dad, an adorable little boy, and a gangly overgrown puppy would not serve her.

In the room next to hers, she heard Kai groaning and getting up. She'd been at rehearsal until late last night, and when she'd heard Marina crying, she'd come in to check on her. Marina had told her everything, and Kai just hugged her.

When Kai married, Marina would miss her, even though they both complained about the noise the other made, just as they had when they were kids.

Marina banged on the wall. "Time to get up, Miss Lazy Bones."

"Go away!"

"Aren't you going to the airport?"

Marina heard another groan and footsteps on the hardwood floors. Kai was up.

Marina grinned and glanced around her bedroom. Living in her old room at her grandmother's home was not where she thought she'd be in her mid-forties, though she'd been grateful for the soft landing when her world blew up. Still, the room was comfortable. Seashells she'd collected from childhood were stowed in large glass pickle jars that sat on a bookcase. An assortment of flip-flops filled a basket by the door.

Her faded summer dresses from years gone by hung in an antique burl wood armoire, and the border of coded symbols Ginger had hand-painted was still firmly attached where the wall met the ceiling. Marina looked up.

To the untrained eye, the decorative border contained what looked like fanciful shapes colorfully rendered in ocean blue, aquamarine, and seafoam green. But it was a cipher, and it had been Ginger's secret message to Marina that she'd had to decode. *Love always triumphs. True love is eternal.* She turned to another portion of the cipher. *As deep as the seas, as wide as the sky, forever through time, my love for you.* Each one of the sisters had their own message.

Brooke had also had a bedroom upstairs, though she had married and moved away long ago. Heather was living there now. Except for a brief period last year when Brooke put her raucous boys and husband on notice by temporarily quitting her job as mother and wife, she hadn't returned to the Coral Cottage as Marina and Kai had. She loved growing vegetables and fruit and could work hours in her organic garden. That was Brooke's private world and métier. With her Birkenstocks and overalls, she was the grounded earth mother of the three sisters.

Lifting her face to the morning breeze wafting through her open window, Marina thought about how much she loved this room that had been her refuge since childhood. But it was time to move on. Jack or no Jack.

The new food truck would turn on the spigot to a new stream of income for her. That would help cover a place of her own if she wanted, along with Heather's remaining college tuition.

Marina picked out a blue-striped sundress and headed toward the shower. Ginger's room was farther down the hallway with a stunning view of the ocean. Regardless of where Bertrand's job had taken them, the couple had kept this beach house and always returned to it.

As Marina splashed cold water onto her puffy face and red eyes, she thought about Kai's friends, who would be arriving soon on an overnight flight from New York. Kai planned to take them to the beach as they were eager to begin their trip with a day in the sun.

After dressing, she made her way to the kitchen. Through the window, she saw Ginger outside picking vegetables in her garden. Marina stepped out to join her.

Ginger looked up expectantly, but when she saw Marina's face, she caught herself. Instead, she held up a loaded stem. "Aren't these heirloom tomatoes stunning this year?"

They were deep red and plump. "The best, I think. Your Anaheim chiles look good, too."

"Help yourself to anything that's ripe," Ginger said lightly. "I've already picked lemons for today."

Marina knew her grandmother was waiting to hear how her date with Jack had gone, but she wasn't ready to talk about it. Instead, Marina focused on plucking the mild, curved green peppers that she used for chile rellenos. She placed them in Ginger's basket.

In an exercise in avoidance, Marina shifted her thoughts

on the day ahead. It was likely that Kai's friends would be hungry when they arrived.

"Those look good."

"That's what I thought," Marina answered, sidestepping Ginger's mild conversational attempt. Marina strolled to a farther plant and focused on recalling the ingredients for her recipe.

But Marina's troubles weren't Ginger's fault. She plucked a few ripe chiles and made her way back to Ginger. "I'll use these for chile rellenos for lunch."

"And how will you make them?"

Marina recognized Ginger's diplomatic skill at diffusing tension. Still, she took her up on it, grateful for some normalcy before she had to launch into the explanation of Jack.

"I'll char the chiles and remove the blackened skin, then lightly stuff them with a blend of white Mexican cheeses. Next, I'll dust them with a hint of flour and fresh oregano and dredge them in beaten egg whites. A quick sauté will set the egg mixture, and I'll finish them in the oven to melt the cheese."

A slow smile rose across Ginger's face. "Served with fresh salsa, that dish will satisfy people without weighing them down. A good choice for the beach."

After carefully flicking a ladybug to another plant, Marina snipped some small-leafed stalks of oregano. Finally, she added an assortment of lettuce to the basket. She looped it over her arm.

As they walked back to the cottage, Marina broke their silence. "I guess you'd like to hear how my dinner with Jack went."

"Only if you want to talk about it."

"He didn't make it." She gave her grandmother a brief explanation.

Ginger raised her brow, a pensive expression on her face.

"I'm sorry you had to go through that. I thought that last night…" Her voice trailed off.

Marina knew what she meant. "So did I. But if we're not meant to be, I won't force it. I have a life to live."

Ginger placed a hand on her arm. "Or he genuinely forgot."

"That would mean he wasn't planning what I thought he was. I was projecting, and while I was disappointed, I understand that I brought that on myself. Maybe it was just dinner."

Ginger nodded sagely. "We must all learn from past mistakes if we are to grow. As much as I like Jack, I support you. You're applying the lessons you learned from Grady. Bravo."

"Then why does it hurt so much?"

Ginger touched her shoulder. "Those are growing pains, my dear. How did you get home last night?"

"A new doctor in town gave me a lift. He's the one taking over Dr. Dede's practice."

A smile touched Ginger's face. "Oh, yes. Jay, I believe. Is he as good-looking as they say?"

"I didn't notice." Marina gave her a conspiratorial grin. "Much," she added.

"Well, then. I'm glad your fabulous new dress and hairstyle weren't wasted. Maybe they were a good investment after all. At the very least, a little competition never hurts."

Her grandmother could always find the positive nuggets. Although her heart still ached, Marina tucked her arm through Ginger's and conjured a smile. "Maybe you're right."

LATER, after making the chile rellenos for Kai and her friends who'd tumbled into the house with a load of luggage and laughter—and for her son Ethan, who was doing some touch-up painting for Ginger today—Marina turned to her preparations for the week.

She wanted to be ahead because this was also the week that Kai and Axe were debuting the new show, *Belles on the Beach*. She'd promised to make picnic box dinners for those who'd placed their orders, and there were quite a few. The Seashell was a hit.

She'd prepared the dry mixture for tomorrow's muffins, which she liked to bake at sunrise, so they were fresh for the farmers market. The chocolate chip cookies, brownies, and tartes were ready as well.

In the morning, she would drop off everything at the booth her sister Brooke now managed. Brooke would arrive early to arrange her organic produce, which Marina purchased from her for the cafe.

Ginger often helped with the prep work for the farmers market, but today was different. With the cottage full of visitors, Marina wanted her grandmother to enjoy their guests. When she'd left them after lunch, Ginger was regaling them with stories about her world travels with Bertrand in the diplomatic service and her friendship with Julia Child. Ginger loved to share and embellish her stories.

That must be where Kai got her love of story-telling and performing.

Satisfied that she'd completed her tasks and was ready for the week ahead, Marina unclipped her hair and shook it out in the ocean breeze that blew through the open window. After shedding her stained chef jacket, she changed back into her sundress and swapped her sturdy closed-toed shoes for a pair of flat sandals she'd worn earlier.

Quickly, she surveyed the compact new kitchen she'd built in the old guest cottage in the back of her grandmother's beach house, making notes for supplies she needed this week.

Before closing the kitchen, she glanced around the space that opened onto a sunny, umbrella-dotted patio that led to the beach to make sure everything was in order. Tomorrow would be busy, but tonight she intended to relax and have fun for Kai's sake.

With or without Jack.

She hadn't reminded him about tonight—he was a grown man, for heaven's sake. Even though she tried to put him out of her mind, she was still upset over the lame excuses he'd given for forgetting their date last night.

Marina pressed her fingers to her pulsing temple and sighed.

The truth was that she cared deeply about Jack. While the logical side of her brain was trying to lead, her heart had another agenda. She'd let down her guard and fallen in love. The passion she'd almost forgotten about had rekindled the glow in her heart.

As these thoughts ricocheted through her mind, another thought occurred to her. What if it was true that Jack was simply embarrassed about having forgotten? Becoming an insta-dad to a half-grown child had certainly been a surprise to him, and he wasn't terribly organized to begin with. She had overlooked a lot because of that.

Still, where should she draw the line?

Just then, she heard footsteps coming toward her.

"Hey, Mom. Sure smells good in here."

Marina glanced up and smiled. Ethan looked so much like his father that she couldn't help thinking how proud Stan would have been of him.

"That sounds like a hint. Are you still hungry?" She knew the answer to that.

Ethan grinned and shook his head. "I wouldn't say no to one for the road. Smells like cookies."

"You have a good nose. Leaving so soon?"

"I finished the painting that Ginger wanted and cleaned up, so I'm going to drive back to San Diego."

"I thought you might stay for supper. I know how you like

to barbecue on the beach, and I'm looking for volunteer chefs."

Ethan laughed. "Not with all of Aunt Kai's friends planning the bridal shower. They're cool, but it's a chick party, if you know what I mean. Besides, I have an early tee time. It's not often I can play the Torrey Pines course, and I need all the practice I can get for the tournament."

"That's okay. I'm impressed with your dedication."

At least she tried. Her son was working toward a career as a professional golfer. Although he hadn't done well in his first year of college due to his problems with dyslexia, he was a naturally gifted golfer.

Marina opened a brown paper bag. "How about some goodies to go? I have muffins and bread, and a tarte you can heat for supper tonight."

Ethan's eyes brightened. "Spinach and mushroom?"

"I know your favorites." She tucked in a spinach, bacon, and mushroom tarte she'd sealed in a take-out container into the bag, along with a loaf of cranberry-orange bread and a handful of oatmeal-raisin cookies.

"Wow, thanks. You're the best, Mom." He slung an arm around her, gave her a hug, and picked up the food. "Did Heather tell you about her possible new internship for the fall?"

"No. Where is it?"

Ethan grinned. "I'd better let her fill you in. She's pretty excited."

As she watched Ethan get into his car and leave, she recalled how busy she'd been with him and his twin sister, Heather. When they'd both left San Francisco to attend Duke University across the country, her life in the city shifted. That was before she'd lost her job and new fiancé on the same day. She'd arrived in Summer Beach at her grandmother's cottage feeling dejected and disheartened at her dismal prospects.

Yet, that had been the beginning of a brand-new life. One that Marina was proud of now.

Heather would be the next to leave. She'd transferred to the less expensive University of California in San Diego when Marina lost her job, insisting that she preferred it anyway. While her daughter often waited tables at the cafe in between classes, it wouldn't be long before she graduated from college.

Marina wondered where Heather would find work. It probably wouldn't be in Summer Beach. Marina would have to look for another server to replace her. Soon, both of her children would be pursuing their dreams out in the big world without her.

She had been looking forward to having Jack and Leo in her life. For all the laughs they'd shared and their intellectual connection, his lack of commitment bothered her. Even if they made up.

She lifted her chin. Then again, she had dreams of her own, including a bright coral-colored food truck just waiting for new adventures.

9

*P*ausing by a mirror before she left her cafe kitchen, Marina smoothed her blue-and-white sundress, dabbed on lip-gloss, and fluffed her new hairstyle. Brandy had done a beautiful job with the shading and long waves.

Feeling better at her age than she had in years, she smiled at her reflection. She was doing what she loved now, and it showed on her face.

Jack or no Jack.

After picking up a plate of cookies she'd made earlier, Marina stepped outside. The summer aromas of warm sand, saltwater, and suntan lotion wafted on the breeze. Beyond the cottage, groups of people lingered on the beach in the sunshine, and the waves lapped the shore.

She strolled across the stone pavers that separated the cafe and its adjoining patios toward the beach house. As she walked, sand crunched beneath the leather soles of her sandals.

The scent of fresh paint lingered in the air, and Marina paused to inspect the front porch that Ethan had touched up with Ginger's signature coral shade.

He's done an excellent job, she thought, pleased that her

son had offered to help when Ginger mentioned it. His father would have liked that, too. As a Marine, Stan had taken his responsibilities seriously.

That's the kind of man she liked.

When Marina approached the house, she could hear laughter spilling from the open windows.

Her youngest sister's friends were lounging on slipcovered furniture in the living room. After spending the day on the beach, they'd gathered at the cottage to throw together plans for Kai's bridal shower. They were sipping the Sunshine Coolers Marina had concocted earlier—a blend of ginger ale with pineapple juice and fresh fruit chunks speared with tiny umbrellas.

Originally, Kai's friends had planned to combine their vacation with her bridal shower planning, but since Kai had moved up the wedding, they were determined to have the party this week. Marina wondered how they were going to manage it. She was providing the food and venue at the cafe, but they were coordinating everything else.

She stepped inside and held up the plate. "Who'd like an oatmeal-raisin cookie?"

"Marina makes the best," Kai said, taking the plate to pass around. "Thanks for these. The coolers are going down pretty easy, too."

Kai and her friends were sprawled around the room, and most still wore their beach coverups. The small group included a few locals from Summer Beach and others from Kai's old theater troupe. An array of bridal magazines and books were spread out before them, and they were working diligently.

Circling the happy mess, Marina asked, "Anyone need another cooler?"

"You should probably bring the pitcher," Kai replied. "And Billie brought some bubbly for the next batch."

Billie brandished a bottle of sparkling Italian wine and

passed it to her. The young, copper-haired woman was one of Kai's friends from New York. Together, they had honed their skills in off-Broadway productions.

Marina had met many of Kai's friends when their touring productions played in San Francisco. Over the years, she's seen them in everything from *Cats* and *Oklahoma!* to *Chicago* and *Mamma Mia*. They were talented, energetic, and quick to laugh and entertain a crowd.

Much like Kai, they were blithe spirits who'd always enjoyed the spotlight.

"I brought a playlist, too." Billie tapped her phone and grinned.

"Bring it on." Kai snapped her fingers to the pop music that filled the room. "Let's get this party started."

Jen, who ran the local hardware store with her husband, turned the pages of a glossy magazine. "What kind of theme should we have?"

Gathering the full skirt of her sundress about her legs, Marina perched on the arm of the canvas slipped-cover couch next to her sister, who was still wearing her scarlet bikini with a leopard-print coverup. "Why don't you surprise her?"

Kai pushed her sunglasses up over her wavy hair. "This is all a surprise to me. Thanks to everyone here," she added with a sweep of her hand.

"I couldn't let you get married without a proper bridal shower," Jen said, clasping her hands around a blue-jeaned knee. She swung her long brown hair over her shoulder. "After all, you hosted one for me."

Marina smiled, glad that Jen had taken the lead. Jen and George were long-time friends of Kai's and owned Nailed It, the local hardware shop next to the Java Beach coffee shop. They had all met years ago when Marina and her sisters visited their grandmother in Summer Beach.

Jen worked almost every day at Nailed It, doling out advice on home renovations. Her father had started the business, and Jen had grown up in it, taking it over after he passed away. If anyone knew how to put together a project, it was Jen.

Another woman sitting cross-legged in a floral coverup, her thick dark hair twisted into a bun, spoke up, "I'll supply flowers and plants." Leilani and her husband Roy Miyake were the proprietors of the Hidden Garden, where Ginger bought all her plants and vegetables for her prized garden. "We could go tropical with pots of orchids and hibiscus or stay traditional with roses and lilies. But if you want prefer cut-flowers, then we should talk to Imani at Blossoms."

While the others talked about decorations and invitations, Marina glanced around the beach cottage. Mexican Talavera pottery flanked the fireplace, and Ginger had bought fresh, bright blue pillows for the white canvas slipcovers she bleached every year. With its worn wooden floors and mementos from Ginger's travels from around the world, this was always a welcome home to Marina. She would actually miss Kai's outbursts of song and sisterly shenanigans, but this had been a temporary landing for both of them.

Thank you, Ginger, she thought. Though their grandmother professed to love having them there, Marina didn't want to overstay her welcome.

She was glad her sister would stay in Summer Beach. If Kai had married the dreadful Dmitri, the man who'd tried to woo her with a diamond the size of a grape, she'd be living in New York, trapped under his authoritarian thumb.

Marina was glad they'd seen the last of him.

After all these years, Kai had finally chosen well. Not that Marina had a better track record, with the exception of Stan, of course.

Jen's voice cut through Marina's thoughts. "And when are we going to throw a shower or a bachelorette party for you, Marina? Java Beach is buzzing about you and Jack."

It was an innocent question, and Marina knew Jen meant

well, but her breath caught in her throat. At a loss for words, she could only shrug.

Kai swiftly cut in, her lilting laugh covering Marina's heartache. "Hey, isn't this my day?" She placed a hand on Marina's knee with a subtle squeeze and shifted the conversation. Tapping a magazine, she wrinkled her nose at it. "That cutesy bridal stuff isn't really me. Let's come up with another theme. Something fun and different."

While Jen, Leilani, and Billie pitched ideas, Marina breathed a sigh of relief and bumped Kai's shoulder. When they were growing up, her youngest sister could be annoying, but she'd always protected Kai. Now that they were older, it worked both ways.

Marina whispered, "Thanks. Love you."

Kai winked and whispered back, "Ditto, kiddo."

While the others talked, Marina thought about the gossip that would soon be zinging around town. Last night's story of Jack standing her up at Beaches was sure to be a hot topic. And she'd left with the hottest new doctor in town. That kind of gossip was too juicy to ignore. She'd have to avoid Java Beach for a while.

Marina drew a hand over her neck, rubbing the tension that had settled in.

She supposed if she was honest with herself, she would have realized that her relationship with Jack had never been on a smooth upward trajectory. He'd been cast against type in this drama. Having been on the professional news treadmill herself, she understood what drove roving investigative journalists like Jack. The thrill of digging into a new story, the adrenaline high from facing down threatening situations—could he leave that behind? Or even, could he afford to?

Moreover, she couldn't ask that of him. One didn't change a tiger's stripes. She turned her attention back to the group, determined to keep her focus on her family this week. After all, this was Kai's special time and she wanted to be there for her.

"How about a beach theme?" Leilani suggested. "We have plenty of decorations for that."

"Or a Broadway theme," Billie said. "Or both. We could wear grass skirts and channel *South Pacific*."

"A Beatles theme could be fun," Jen mused. "George and I saw *Beatlemania* in New York, and Axe sang 'Yesterday' at our wedding. Wow, what a voice he has."

"These are all good ideas." Kai sounded excited.

Billie's eyes lit with another idea. "How about Broadway's greatest love stories?"

"*Phantom of the Opera*." Kai threw back her strawberry blond hair and drew a theatrical hand across her brow. "I love every song in that musical, even if it has been overdone."

"Or 'Helpless' from *Hamilton*," Billie said, growing excited.

Others joined in with more Broadway tune suggestions while Jen took notes.

Marina was getting into the mood now. "How about 'Suddenly Seymour?' from *Little Shop of Horrors*?"

Kai and her friends roared with laughter. Her sister wagged her finger at her. "This is why you're not on the entertainment committee. But I love you, Sis." She flung her arms around Marina.

Jen held up her hands. "We have a lot of great ideas. Why don't we make a program right now, put out the emergency call to friends, and see who wants to sing what? Kai, can we raid your costume department?"

"Of course." Kai clapped her hands. "Honestly, no one has to bring a gift if they don't feel like it. This isn't about that old-fashioned gift-grab notion. I just want my gal pals and guy friends together having a good time. Can't we do that?"

Marina slung her arm over Kai's shoulder. "You always have to do things your way, don't you?"

Kai threw her head back and laughed. "I guess I do. Won't this be fun?"

Everyone broke out with laughter and began talking about their new plan.

As much as Marina wanted Kai to have her picture-perfect bridal shower and wedding, this approach fit her sister and reflected her passions. That's what a union of two souls should be, she thought.

Happy that they'd made a decision, Marina carried Billie's prosecco to the kitchen, where Ginger was seated at a red Formica table. Although the kitchen was dated, everything was exceptionally well cared for. The fire engine red O'Keefe & Merritt stove from the 1960s was polished to perfection. Marina had learned to cook with her grandmother at that stove. Her kitten-heeled sandals tapped on the terracotta Saltillo tile floor.

Ginger wore a cotton wrap dress in a vivid shade of mint green that accented her trim figure and hair. Discreet pearls graced her earlobes. Her posture was erect, as always, giving her a commanding presence that belied her age. A teacup sat in front of her, and she leaned forward with interest. "It sounds like Kai's shower is underway."

"And just in time."

"That's our Kai. Always full of last-minute surprises." Ginger eyed her. "So, how are you doing?"

When Marina didn't reply right away, Ginger gave her a sympathetic smile. "I heard what Jen said, too. Unfortunately, people will talk and speculate. Not her, of course. But your sisters and I are here for you."

"I know how much you like and admire Jack," Marina said, feeling her chest tighten with fresh disappointment. "But honestly, I don't know if he's right for me."

10

*W*ith Kai's bridal shower on track, Marina had plenty to focus on besides Jack. Now that she would have the food truck this week, she added *order supplies* and *schedule staff* to her mental list. Jack might have disappointed her, but she had to redirect her energy.

Leaning over the kitchen sink, she opened Billie's bottle of prosecco to avoid the potential fizzy overflow from the woman's enthusiastic handling.

"People make mistakes," Ginger said, sipping her tea at the kitchen table. "The question is why Jack did, and can you live with that? At heart, I believe he's still a good man. Maybe out of his element, though."

While Marina was through with the topic of Jack, Ginger was clearly pressing on. Feeling slightly annoyed, she said, "While I appreciate your wisdom, what if marriage is outside of his element, too?" She poured a small amount of prosecco into a glass to taste it.

"Is that really such a deal breaker?" Ginger asked thoughtfully. When Marina didn't answer, she went on, her eyes taking on a steely glint. "I might be of a certain age, but I'm modern enough to realize not every couple should be married or merge assets. For example, a woman should not endanger her financial position after a certain age merely for what she thinks is love. I've seen far too many good-looking gigolos siphon a woman's retirement account."

Shocked, Marina spewed out the prosecco. Wiping her chin, she asked, "Is that what you think Jack is?" That thought hadn't occurred to her.

"Not at all, but if you move on, you must be aware of what's out there, especially since you're building a valuable business." Ginger paused, peering at her. "Perhaps companionship is the answer."

Marina leaned against the kitchen counter, considering the question. She hadn't thought about that, though it could be a solution that would work for some people.

Still, Marina shook her head. "If I'm going to be involved with Jack, or any man, I want to know where I stand. And that we're moving forward and creating a life in partnership with the same values and goals. For me, that means marriage. Jack might not be up for that."

Ginger weighed her reply, then said, "Just so you know that you have options as a woman."

"You bet I do," Marina said sharply.

Her grandmother gave her a sympathetic look. "Right now, you're hurt, embarrassed, and justifiably upset about last night. You must talk to him. Make sure you're in agreement going forward, or you're just wasting each other's time."

Marina sighed. Once again, her grandmother was correct. Marina was hurt, and an ache grew in her heart even as Ginger spoke. What had happened to the prince she'd thought he was? That had been her self-deception, she supposed. Marina picked up the bottle. "That's easier to say than manage."

"I'm only looking out for you." Ginger inclined her head. "He and Leo will be at the barbecue tonight, won't they?"

"I have no idea, but I'm not going to remind him."

Marina motioned toward Kai and her friends in the living room. "I don't want my troubles to put a damper on this party. This is Kai's moment."

"And Kai would like nothing more than to see you happy —however you define that." Ginger lifted the steaming tea to her lips.

Feeling she might have spoken a little harshly, Marina added, "I appreciate your advice." She grinned. "Gigolos and all." What would she ever do without Ginger?

Her grandmother's eyes twinkled over the teacup.

Marina stopped and stared at the thin porcelain cup Ginger held. The 19th-century teacup was embellished with strokes of gold and pale pink, hand-painted roses. *Likely from Limoges, France.* Her grandmother often rotated her treasures to enjoy them all. Suddenly, Marina recalled something she'd read and frowned.

"Do you think you should be concerned about the lead content of that porcelain? Maybe you should limit it to decorative use."

Ginger lifted an expertly tinted eyebrow. "Darling, living well hasn't killed me yet."

"But—"

Her grandmother put the teacup down. "We all have an expiry date. So do you, as hard as it might be to fathom that at your age."

"What?" Marina choked out the word. She was appalled at the matter-of-fact way Ginger put it, but that was her way, especially when there was no avoiding the issue.

Ginger only shrugged a shoulder still well-toned from yoga. "I suggest you be more concerned about living your life well. One chance, that's all we have, dear. As far as we know, that is. Remind me to check into that fascinating cryonic—"

"You've always said," Marina cut in, not wanting to go into *that* subject. Freezing her grandmother? She shuddered.

"The more we know, the better we can do. And your health—"

"Is still my concern. I manage it well." With a motion of graceful resignation, Ginger indicated the teapot on the counter. "That said, you may pour a different cup for me if it makes you feel better." She pushed the offending china aside. "And you're probably right. I did read a scientific study about that."

Concealing her smile, Marina reached for the newer teacup. Her grandmother had always been one to embrace change. Perhaps that was her nature, or maybe it was her intellectual training. And yet, the conversation unnerved her. Would Ginger conceal a health problem to protect her grand-daughters?

"As for your health," Ginger went on, a smile dancing on her lips. "Come with me on a hike to the ridgetop. Morning yoga overlooking the sea is magnificent."

Marina shook off her thoughts. She wasn't sure she could manage that hike herself, so if Ginger was healthy enough to scale a cliff and continue her yoga practice, she must be fine. "I need to work up to that."

"I'll hold you to it," Ginger said with a wink.

Marina reached for a lemon from a colorful Talavera pottery bowl on the counter. Deftly, she drew a knife through the fresh fruit Ginger had picked this morning, then placed a slice beside the new cup of tea she'd poured.

As she placed the fresh tea in front of Ginger, laughter bubbled from the living room again. Kai deserved to have all the giggly fun with her friends that she wanted. She wanted this party—and Kai's wedding, whenever that would be—to be all her sister had dreamed of.

Only seven years separated Marina and Kai, but it often seemed like a generation. Life could do that to you. She nodded toward the living room. "They're making me feel old."

"Nonsense." Ginger straightened, lifting her chin. "You're still young. And I'm feeling younger than ever. Have Heather and that new cook you hired take over for a day and spend it with me. I'll teach you the art of living well. A hike and yoga, then a massage and a good lunch. What's good for the body is good for the mind."

"Is that your secret?"

"One of many."

Marina knew her grandmother would enjoy having a day off together, but when would she ever have the time? "Maybe I will."

Ginger tapped the table. "Then why the furrowed brow?"

She motioned to the glasses. "I have to make these coolers—"

"They can wait. In fact, pour one for yourself and sit with me for a moment. I think you're still in shock after last night."

After filling a small glass with ginger ale and pineapple juice and adding lime zest, Marina took a seat at the table she remembered from childhood.

"Not that long ago, I was a well-coiffed, high-heeled news anchor in San Francisco covering hard news. Now I run a beach cafe on my grandmother's property, wear clogs, and serve food with a side of local gossip."

"Sounds like you're winning to me."

"But I never expected such drastic changes in my mid-forties."

"Jack aside, perhaps you're having a mid-life crisis, which I prefer to call a readjustment. Something we should do at least every decade. I think you were overdue."

Marina laughed. "Maybe I am. I just bought a screaming yellow food truck."

"Which is a wise investment in your future." Ginger sipped her tea, then set it down on a saucer and leveled an appraising gaze at her. Even at her age, she still had the sharp, strategic mind of a master chess player.

As Marina shifted, her chair squeaked under the silent scrutiny. She took a gulp of her drink.

Ginger touched her hand. "Just because this is Kai's big event doesn't minimize your journey. Both of you are embarking on new lives."

"Kai is way ahead of me."

"Is it a race, dear?"

"Of course not." Marina traced a scratch on the table. "I want Kai to have the wedding of her dreams. I just wish she'd tell us what they are. Besides, I'm not sure my goals are aligned with Jack's after all."

Ginger reached for her hand and smiled. "Maybe they're not. But I also want to add that what we spend precious time worrying about rarely comes to pass. As long as we are pursuing our passions in a positive manner, life has a way of unfolding naturally. It's quite surprising."

Marina shook her head. "I can't make any more mistakes. Not at my age."

"Trust the process for a little while." Ginger laughed. "And whether you realize it or not, you have plenty of time to make any number of mistakes. Just make sure you're having fun when you do."

Marina grinned. "And protect my assets."

"Never actually marry the gigolo." Ginger winked and lifted her tea to her lips.

"Has anyone ever told you that you're incorrigible?"

"I'll take that as a fine compliment."

Marina laughed. Maybe Ginger was right, and she'd been overthinking life. As the sound of Beyonce's "Single Ladies" thumped from the living room, Marina shook off her thoughts.

Just then, her phone buzzed in her pocket. Withdrawing it, she stared at the text, her spirits rising. "Listen to this. Judith says she has the sale paperwork ready, and she can deliver the food truck soon. This means I'll have to train my team and start marketing and planning routes." Ideas bubbled in her mind.

"Someday you could have an entire fleet of trucks."

Marina liked that idea. "Maybe so. Or I could create a concept to replicate them."

"Franchising is interesting." Admiration flickered in her grandmother's eyes. "I'm always happy to help you sort through concepts."

"I'd like that very much."

Marina drained her cooler and stepped to the counter. She poured part of the prosecco into the pitcher and added an equal part of pineapple juice.

Thinking about her fresh plans, she stared from the kitchen window toward the horizon while the vista of a new future shimmered ahead in her mind.

She had struggled so much in the past. Even though Heather had transferred to a less expensive school, living in San Francisco with the twins had been costly. Marina had juggled bills for dental, medical, clothing, and tuition—everything times two at once. She had never managed to get a toehold in home ownership in the city or save much.

Marina couldn't depend on Jack—or any man, for that matter. If anyone would have stuck by her, it would have been Stan. Circumstances beyond her control could occur, and she had to look out for herself. No one was going to do it for her, not even Ginger.

Besides, Marina wanted her grandmother to have plenty for the best comfort and care she might need as she grew older. At what Marina hoped was the midpoint in her life, she had to grasp chances while she still had the energy.

She added sprigs of mint as a garnish and lifted the pitcher. "I'd better see to that parched, raucous party in there and then start preparing for the barbecue."

Ginger looked up from the table. "Will we have many tonight?"

Marina paused by the doorway. Jen and Leilani's husbands were joining them. "The guys are coming after work. Axe, George, and Roy. And Brooke called to say that she and Chip are bringing the boys."

"It will be wonderful to see everyone," Ginger said.

Neither of them mentioned Jack.

11

"*More* s'mores coming right up." Marina twirled a slim wire basket over a fire on the beach, trying to keep her gaze off Jack. Much to her consternation, he'd had the nerve to show up with Leo and Scout after standing her up last night.

She glanced around the fire, where her family and friends were roasting skewered marshmallows to a blackened crisp. The sweet scent of marshmallows, toasted graham crackers, and melted chocolate rose on the ocean breeze, along with the sounds of laughter and chatter. They'd all pitched in to bring beach chairs, blankets, and coolers.

Kai and Axe were the guests of honor. Many of their friends were gathered around, including Jen and George, Leilani and Roy, and Kai's friends who were visiting from New York and Los Angeles. Shelly from the Seabreeze Inn and Mitch, the proprietor of Java Beach, had also joined the party. Marina's friend Ivy was there, along with Bennett. He'd brought his guitar and was strumming it softly. Kai hummed along, singing a few lines as the music inspired her.

Across from them, her grandmother sat in her beach chair like an empress on her throne, taking it all in. Her dark denims and white cotton shirt were crisply pressed, and she wore a jaunty length of vintage silk at her throat. Marina recognized the scarf as one that Ginger had bought years ago in Paris, where her late husband had been stationed as a diplomat.

Even their middle sister Brooke and her husband had joined them. Their three boys had been playing with Leo on the beach. Brooke sat next to Ginger now, catching up and sharing updates about the boys.

Only Ethan and Heather were missing. Her son had his early tee time, and her daughter had a summer social that she'd organized with her friends at college.

Marina had been shocked when Jack and Leo arrived. And to her even greater surprise, Jack had come prepared to build a fire and roast hot dogs and other food he'd brought.

So, she let him, although she felt a little guilty for taking perverse pleasure in allowing him to work himself back into her good graces. But only a little. He'd have to do much more than that to earn a place in her life.

Marina wondered if Ginger might have had something to do with his prompt appearance. Or maybe he figured he should shape up. She slid a glance in his direction.

"Need some help there?" Jack asked, moving closer.

"I've got this." Although it was a balmy beach evening, his nearness sent shivers through Marina. Even in a worn T-shirt and threadbare jeans, he was still attractive to her. To counter that, she focused on what she was doing.

"There's a trick to s'mores," she explained, a cold edge creeping into her voice. "You have to turn them evenly, or all the gooey goodness oozes into the fire."

"Really, I can help."

"Thanks, but you grilled most of our supper." Whether Ginger was behind this new attitude or not, Marina wasn't ready to forgive him just yet.

Jack flashed a grin in the firelight. "Grilling dinner wasn't so tough."

"Then how about constructing more of these?" She tossed a bag of marshmallows onto his lap. Although she had to admit, he'd done more than jab and grill a few hot dogs. To her surprise, he was quite competent over an open flame.

Jack opened the bag. "Got it. Leo, will you give me a hand?"

"Sure." In the firelight, the boy's profile mirrored his father's, right down to the thick, tousled hair brushed back from his forehead.

They both needed a good haircut. Jack probably couldn't be bothered. Without meaning to, she let out a puff of exasperation. Hastily, she added, "Don't forget the chocolate."

Jack gave her a look of amusement. "We won't. We'll get a regular s'mores production line going for you."

Marina tried not to smile as he and Leo focused on constructing the dessert just as she had, layering slivers of dark, orange-flavored chocolate and puffy marshmallows over the crispy graham cracker slabs. Unable to stand how adorable Leo was being with his father, she tore her gaze from them.

Nothing but trouble there, she told herself.

Across the flickering yellow flames, Kai lounged on a beach blanket. Axe had his arm draped across her shoulders, gazing at his fiancée as if she were the brightest star in the sky. Leaning against Axe's solid chest, Kai looked enraptured, too.

Marina's heart ached at this sweet, romantic scene. She smiled at them, silently willing their union to last through the challenges life would inevitably throw in their path. Kai deserved every good thing she'd worked for. She had waited years for a good man who shared her interests, not just a fan or tech playboy who wanted a dazzling trophy on his arm.

There had been plenty of those.

Marina continued sweeping the basket over the flames,

toasting the edges of the graham crackers and melting the dark chocolate and creamy marshmallow inside.

Jack nodded toward the basket she was using. "That contraption works well."

"It's good to know the tricks of the trade."

Throwing his arm around his son, Jack pulled the boy close. "We're both learning. Leo wants us to sign up for your Saturday cooking classes."

Seriously? She arched an eyebrow at him. "You don't need to do that."

"We all know that's a lie." Jack chuckled and shook his head.

The firelight illuminated Jack's strong features, bathing his face in a warm glow. He was acting at ease, but Marina detected an undercurrent—as if he wasn't ready to share something yet. Maybe there was more to the reason he hadn't shown up last night than he'd let on.

Yet, if they still had a chance at a future together, they would need trust and transparency between them.

In the firelight, Jack's eyes shimmered with fierce intelligence, and Marina watched him register every detail about those around the fire and on the beach. Following his gaze, she saw that he was watching Kai and Axe with interest, too.

Deciding to chip away at the ice between them, Marina leaned toward him. "Everyone liked your ground turkey and vegetables. My mother used to prepare those little foil packages for campfires, too." He'd even brought his own seasoning mixture, which surprised her, and when he began preparing them, she'd left him alone in the kitchen. "Even Ginger thought that was delicious." She sat back, satisfied with herself. She'd made an effort.

Jack shrugged with modesty but seemed pleased by the compliment and conversation. "Glad I can still handle spearing hotdogs and roasting corn. It wasn't in the same league as your creations, but food always tastes better on the beach with friends and cold libations. I missed that when I was living in New York, even though the street meat was pretty good. Especially late at night."

"Isn't barbecuing practically an Olympic sport in Texas?"

Jack grinned. "When I was growing up, cooking over a campfire and handling the barbecue were rites of passage for most young men. I don't know how it is today."

"But not finding the door to the kitchen?" Marina lifted her brow, teasing him.

"That was my mother's domain." Jack hung his head a little. "I know it sounds unfair, but dad and I worked the farm. Now I wish I'd learned more from her before it was too late."

She was actually impressed by how he'd managed the cookout—with a little help from Mitch. As inept as Jack was in the kitchen, he was better with what had started out as almost a bonfire. They'd had to wait for the fire to die down, but once it did, Jack proved he could grill with the best. She'd prepared kebobs that afternoon, but she'd promptly turned them over to Jack.

He bumped Leo's shoulder. "Wish you'd had a chance to know your grandmother, son. I'll show you photos someday."

With a face smudged with chocolate, Leo looked up. "When can I meet my cousins? Samantha has some she hangs out with sometimes."

Lifting an edge of his mouth in a thoughtful quirk, Jack nodded. "You'll meet them soon."

"Who wants another s'more?" Marina called out, trying to extricate herself from Jack and Leo. She wasn't ready to yield to them yet.

Kai held up her plate. "I'll take that one."

Axe tickled her side. "Where do you put all that?"

Laughing, Kai thumped her fiancé's shoulder. "I dance it off in every show. Or haven't you noticed?"

"I notice everything about you, sweetheart," Axe replied, kissing Kai's cheek.

Kai and Axe had been performing several shows a week at their new amphitheater. Lately, they'd been immersed in rehearsals for the new production, and Marina could hardly wait to see it.

"Kai is our Lady of Perpetual Motion," Axe said, massaging her shoulders.

"Hey, what about me?" Leo asked.

Behind him, Scout perked up his ears.

"I have another pair of s'mores coming right up," Marina said. "But only for you, Leo. Chocolate is bad for dogs. Like hot sauce."

Jack winced. "Ouch."

Scout yelped as if in protest, and Leo picked up a piece of driftwood. With all his little-boy might, he hurled it for the dog to retrieve. Scout took off, stretching his legs across the sand.

Marina's life had changed the moment Jack had arrived in Summer Beach with his new puppy in tow and met the son he'd never known he had. Despite their rift, Marina still adored Leo. Jack freely admitted his son was the best part of him.

Right now, she couldn't agree more.

Ginger leaned toward the fire, warming her hands. "Summer has always been the season of weddings in Summer Beach." Nodding to her granddaughters, she began a story. "Your parents married on this very beach, surrounded by family and friends." She gestured to a large flat rock that jutted toward the sea. "Right there. That's where they exchanged vows. Isn't that a perfect spot?"

As Kai shifted to look at the spot, her lips lifted in a thoughtful expression, and she sighed. "I can just imagine."

"That was our mermaid queen rock," Marina said. "We used to play there."

"How about having your wedding there?" Ginger asked.

Kai and Axe exchanged an amused look. "We'll let you know," Kai replied.

Marina couldn't help wondering if they might be planning to elope. For Ginger's sake, she hoped not.

While everyone chatted about other recent weddings, Marina continued turning the s'mores. This summer, she had hosted more engagement parties, rehearsal dinners, and wedding celebrations at the Coral Cafe than she could count. She had hired extra people who worked busy shifts and special events. They were so talented and personable that she hated the thought of letting them go at the end of the summer, especially since they needed the work.

Now, with the new food truck, she might not have to.

Her sister's engagement ring dazzled against the flickering flames, catching Marina's attention. She was truly happy for Kai.

Jack also noticed the blazing ruby surrounded by diamonds.

Marina wondered what was going through his mind. She slid another look at him. It was just as well this way, she decided. She didn't want to steal the limelight from Kai. But if she and Jack were to continue dating, she needed to know that her time was well invested. Maybe she was old-fashioned, but marriage meant a lot to her.

So did proper proposals.

Leo bounced in anticipation. "Is mine ready yet?"

"Almost, and these are the best yet." As Marina turned the wire mesh basket over the flames, she gazed around their circle of family and friends who languished on blankets and beach chairs, relaxed and satisfied after the food they'd had.

Bennett was strumming an old Beatles tune, "Yesterday." Axe picked up the tune, serenading Kai with his low baritone.

As Kai listened to Axe, her face—sun-kissed and devoid of makeup—glowed in the flickering light. Marina thought she'd never seen Kai look more lovely. That's what love did to people.

Her sister might have enjoyed performing with the touring

theater company, but Summer Beach had always held her heart. Now that she and Axe were running the local theater, Kai had everything she wanted here. So did Axe. As he finished the song, he gave Kai a soft kiss.

Marina's heart melted for them. And that wasn't all. She jerked the wire basket from the flames.

"Careful, the chocolate is dripping." Quickly, Jack handed her a napkin.

"Thanks." Deftly, she slid the toasted s'mores onto a plate and passed them to Leo. "Here you are, sport. Careful, they're hot." She turned to Jack. "Do you have more ready?"

Jack reached for the marshmallows. "Hang on. I got behind listening to Axe and Bennett."

Kai clapped her hands. "Well, pick up the pace, cowboy. We don't get to do this very often."

Jack chuckled. "It's been a long time since I've been called that."

"Face it, you're a beach bum now," Axe said. "You're right where you belong here in Summer Beach. Right, Marina?"

Marina pressed her lips together. Axe probably didn't know what had happened between them, so she let it pass.

As for Jack, she wasn't sure if he would agree with Axe about belonging here. He'd blown in on the ocean breeze, a writer who could work anywhere, and he had for many years. As a renter, he could pick up and leave tomorrow if he wanted, especially now that Vanessa was well enough to care for Leo again.

Would he actually want to call Summer Beach home?

However, glancing around the fire at her family and friends, Marina was certain that she was exactly where she belonged. She didn't want to miss these years with her grandmother. Ginger was the only link to their family history, and Marina still had much to learn from her.

Someday, Marina would be the matriarch of the Delavie-Moore family, and it would be her responsibility to carry on the history. She dreaded the day they would lose Ginger—she didn't like to think of that at all.

A cool ocean breeze scattered a stack of napkins, and Brooke's children scrambled after them. The wind tousled Jack's hair, too. As he swept it back, his arm casually brushed hers.

Marina's chest tightened at his closeness. After mourning the death of her first husband, she'd doubted the chance of finding love again. Yet, she'd been wrong. Jack had cracked her heart wide open. Now it lay exposed and wounded. She had to guard it carefully.

"Here's another one for you." Oblivious to her thoughts, Jack leaned toward her. He flipped open the hot mesh basket with the edge of his T-shirt, which already bore stripes of black char, and eased the treats inside. Shadows from the fire danced across his face.

She caught her breath. "Don't hurt yourself."

A slow smile spread across Jack's face.

"Jack is tougher than he looks," Axe said.

"Women are far tougher," Kai interjected as she waited for her dessert to cool. "We're the ones having babies and juggling families and careers." She tapped Axe's chest. "Like Ginger Rogers and Fred Astaire, I do everything he does, but backwards and in high heels."

"I'll admit there's a lot to that," Axe said, laughing. "But I promise you, we'll be a team at home and on the stage."

Kai winked at him. "I'll be sure to remember you said that after we get married." She turned to Ginger. "By the way, I'm going to need that 'something old' for the wedding soon."

"I thought you might," Ginger said. "I have a trove of treasures in the attic."

Kai's eyes shimmered with interest. "I'd love to see what else you have up there."

Last December, they had raided Ginger's attic for the holiday performance—*A Christmas Carol at the Beach*—that Kai and Axe had put on at their new amphitheater. Marina recalled the night Axe had proposed onstage to Kai. Magic was truly in the air—for them, and for her and Jack. What a perfect night it had been. If only…

Leo had been listening intently, and now he turned to Jack. "Dad, when are you and Marina getting married?"

Marina held her breath.

Around the fire, everyone stared at Jack, waiting for his reply.

Caught off-guard, Jack bobbled a marshmallow and sent it careening into the fire, where it promptly sizzled, charred in the flames. "Well, we might not be at that, uh…that stage anymore."

He cast a look at Marina and lowered his voice. "I messed up, and I'm really sorry. You deserved much better. From the depths of my heart, I hope you can forgive me."

After a slight hesitation, Marina nodded. His apology sounded sincere.

"But Dad, you told me you loved her."

Leo wasn't letting this go. Marina swallowed against a lump in her throat while soft laughter rippled around the fire.

Seeing Leo's crestfallen face, Marina felt sorry for the boy. All he wanted was to have those he loved around him. *And a sense of home.* She understood.

Jack stumbled over his words again. "I don't think she… you understand, right, Leo?"

As Jack's voice trailed off, Marina wondered if she should jump in to assist, but feeling her grandmother's eyes on her, she decided not to rescue Jack.

Actually, they were sort of cute. Watching Leo's earnest expression and Jack's discomfort, Marina smothered a laugh.

Suddenly, Leo's eyes flashed with inspiration, and he grinned broadly. "Dad, don't be embarrassed. I've got this." Arranging a serious look on his chocolate-smeared face, the boy turned to her. "Marina, will you marry us?"

Marina's heart lurched, and she nearly dropped the s'mores into the flames. This was not what she'd expected.

"Whoop, whoop!" Kai exclaimed, clapping. "You go, Leo!"

Axe let out a deep guffaw. "Got to admit, the kid's got guts."

"More than his dad," Mitch added, slapping his knee.

Jack's face grew red at the comments, and he drew a hand over his chin. "Son, that's a big step."

"That's what Mom said. But she was ready to get married, and I think we are, too." Leo beamed at Marina, waiting for her answer.

Jack put a hand on Leo's arm. "You can't just ask a woman to marry you. I mean, marry us."

Leo raised his shoulders in a shrug. "But I just did."

More laughter bubbled around the circle of friends.

Across the flickering flames, Ginger was clearly amused, though she spoke with great seriousness. "It's not every day a woman receives such a fine invitation. Marina, you should consider this young man's request very carefully."

"Yeah, Dad. See?" Leo ramped up his focus on Marina. "You'd be with us all the time. It would be great. I promise to keep my room sort of clean. I can feed Scout, too, because Dad sometimes forgets."

Marina smiled. "Why am I not surprised at that?"

Brooke nodded toward the rock where their parents were married. "You could have a double wedding ceremony right there on the beach. Imagine, marrying off both my sisters at once. Wouldn't that be fun?"

Ginger's eyes darted to Brooke with approval. "What a sensible solution for our family and friends. They'll appreciate that."

This was getting out of hand, and Marina sensed Jack's discomfort. "Oh, Brooke, I don't think—"

"What a splendid idea." Ginger cut in and raised her hands to Kai and Marina.

Holding the s'mores aloft, Marina gaped at her grand-mother. Had she and Leo planned this? That was an outlandish thought, but wasn't all of this?

Everyone started talking at once, crowding Marina's thoughts. Pressure built in her head.

"Ouch," she cried, getting her hand too close to the fire. She dropped the s'mores on a plate. "Oh, y*eesey Louisey!*" She shook her burned finger, biting back more colorful words.

Leo whipped around to his father. "Did you hear that? I think she said *yes.*" The boy bounced a couple of times. "She said *yes,* Dad!"

Jack looked befuddled. "I heard you, kiddo."

It took Marina a moment to realize Leo didn't understand what she'd meant—or maybe he hadn't heard her correctly with everyone else talking. She hated to disappoint the boy. "Oh, Leo, I'd really like nothing better—"

"For real?" Jack asked, his hoarse voice barely above a whisper. He took her burned finger and softly kissed it.

The tender movement drew Marina in, and she longed to take Jack in her arms and make up the hurt they were both feeling. Yet, what would her children think? She and Heather and Ethan had always been a tight trio, and they still were. "Shouldn't we talk about this?"

"That's what we're doing." Jack's voice was edged with raw emotion. "Maybe it's awkward, but…I've been thinking about it. Very seriously." He squeezed her other hand in a hopeful motion.

"I—" Marina stopped. She gazed between these two who had such a hold on her heart. Right now, that heart was wildly thumping blood throughout her body, rendering her a little light-headed. Maybe Jack *had* intended to propose last night.

Leo's eyes glittered with excitement.

Never taking his eyes from her, Jack kissed her hand,

waiting.

Across the flickering flames, Kai egged her on, while Ginger's impenetrable stare seized her.

"Yes," Marina blurted out, surprising even herself.

Leo tugged his father's arm. "Dad, did you hear that again? She wants to marry us!"

The boy's delight sliced through the tension, and Jack laughed.

"So it seems. Good work, kid." Jack embraced Marina and whispered into her ear. "I guess this is official."

"Well, sure."

Marina was painfully aware that she sounded as uncertain as he did. And yet, why should she be? She loved Jack, despite his imperfections. In her heart, she felt this was right, even if it was Leo who had proposed.

Ginger pushed forward in her chair. "Kai, darling, would you and Axe fetch my good champagne in the refrigerator in the bar? And bring my best crystal for them."

Kai pushed to her feet. "We have plenty of plastic cups."

Ginger shot her a withering look. "And a proper flute for me. We have to celebrate this momentous decision."

"Alrighty then, champagne and s'mores for everyone," Kai cried, waving her arms above her head.

Leo grinned. "Even me?"

"Ginger ale for you, sport." Jack brought his son into a hug with Marina. Even Scout raced to join them.

With their arms around her and Scout intent on licking her face, Marina thought it was all wild and impetuous, and not at all how she had imagined it would be, but this was real. And she had never felt more loved than at that moment.

She gazed into Jack's eyes, which were misted with emotion. Though he looked as shocked as she felt, this was the man she loved. Of that, Marina was certain.

She only hoped her twins would understand this sudden decision.

12

"*A*sking Marina to marry us was pretty gutsy of you," Jack said, tousling Leo's hair with one hand as he steered the VW van along the coastal road with the other.

After her acceptance last night, he had been so elated it had taken time to wind down and close his eyes. Today, Jack was surfing rainbows of happiness.

"Why, Dad? Everyone else is getting married, and when people love each other, they get married." He kicked his feet on the floorboards, which were covered with a fine sandy silt. "That's what you said about Mom and Dr. Noah."

"So I did. Way to go, little man. Awfully proud of you." He held up his hand for a high-five.

Leo slapped his father's hand and gave him a wide grin, revealing a couple of empty spaces with missing baby teeth farther back. "I think I'll ask Samantha to get married."

Jack frowned. "Wait a minute, sport. You guys are still pretty young. Give it a few years. College first, kiddo."

"I know that." Leo tried to roll his eyes, but instead, his lids just fluttered.

Jack suppressed a laugh. Leo was still working on his technique, but he would probably have it perfected by the time he was a teenager. "Where'd you learn that?"

"What?"

"That eye roll you're working on."

"Friends from school, I guess." Leo gave an equally elaborate shrug and stared out the window at the passing scenery. They were hugging the beach, and Leo liked to watch the ocean for migrating whales and dolphins.

"Figures." His son was practically a pre-teen, though Jack wasn't sure exactly what age that was.

Still, Jack knew these were crucial years with his son. Vanessa was an amazing mother, and he didn't want to mess up anything with his son. He figured he had only a few years before Leo no longer thought of his father as a rock star. He was already starting to see changes in him, but that was part of growing up.

At least he'd gotten to spend this part of Leo's childhood with him. For that, Jack was grateful. He still wished Vanessa would have told him about Leo sooner, but he understood her reasons. They hadn't had a real relationship, and he wasn't father material back then. Besides, her father might have killed him.

Not literally, of course. That is, he didn't think so. Though Jack liked to think he could have won him over if he'd had to.

Even so, Jack was happy for Vanessa now. She and Dr. Noah were meant for each other, and he hoped they were enjoying their honeymoon. This would be the longest time he'd had with Leo.

Jack had a good situation here in Summer Beach. No way was he giving this up, especially since he and Marina were officially engaged. That was more reason to move forward with purchasing the cottage he'd been renting, even if it was a unique property.

He'd become accustomed to the ocean mural in the living room and the palm tree painted in the kitchen. Leo loved the undersea mural in his bedroom. They'd been painted with love by the former owner, an accomplished artist. He hoped Marina would feel the same way about the artwork.

"Are we almost there yet?"

Jack laughed. "Is that from the *Official Kid's Handbook*?"

"The what?"

"Never mind. We're here." He turned into the Fisherman's Wharf parking lot, which was a dirt patch off the road. "Freshest seafood in town. This is where the fishing vessels come in. We can catch a ride sometime and go out with them if you want. Or drop a line over on that side."

Leo bounced in his seat. "That would be cool."

This morning, Bennett had asked Jack to meet him there to talk about the house. The mayor said he had city business at the wharf, so they could meet for lunch if Jack was free. He was, and he made sure it was all right that he brought Leo along.

The sun was warm on Jack's shoulders as he and Leo walked along the wooden pier, where bait shops and tourist gift shops stood side by side. At the end of the short pier was Mel's Fish, reputed to be the best casual dining place for fresh fish in Summer Beach.

The chalkboard outside listed the menu and the fresh catch of the day. Fish-and-chips was the specialty, plus tuna poke, mahi-mahi fish tacos, clam chowder, mussels, and so much more. They even had burgers and vegetarian options.

"Looks like our kind of place, Leo." Jack stepped inside, the worn boards creaking beneath his feet. Double doors stood open to the deck outside, which overlooked the water.

Bennett sat at a table on the deck with a gray-haired man who looked a little older than they were.

The mayor waved toward him, and Jack and Leo made their way to the table. He introduced the other man. "Garrett grew up in the house you're living in."

"It's a real pleasure meeting you." Jack had been sending

his rent to a post office box, with the checks made out to a trust. "My son Leo and I love your house." They shook hands and sat down at the wooden table.

Garrett folded his hands and peered at Leo with twinkling eyes. "Tell me, son, do you like the underwater mural in your room?"

Leo's eyes widened. "I sure do. Sometimes I pretend that's me scuba diving."

"My father painted that for me," Garrett said, chuckling. "He made sure to include my favorite creatures in the scene. Let's see, if memory still serves me, there were orange-and-white striped clownfish, some bright yellow and blue tangs, and a scary striped lionfish. He even added an octopus I named Ollie."

"And what about friendly lobster?" Leo said, his eyes widening.

"How could I forget?" Garrett laughed. "That lobster waved to me every morning."

"Are you the one who became an oceanographer?" Jack asked.

"That's right, and I just retired. It was only my father and me. Sort of like you and your son, I understand."

Maybe that explained why the vintage, blue enamel oven still looked new, Jack thought.

Just then, a server brought three glasses of iced tea and a lemonade for Leo. They ordered lunch—four fish-and-chips, the lunchtime specialty.

While they were waiting for their food, Bennett leaned forward. "I talked to Garrett about your desire to buy the house, and he's willing to sell it."

"Great," Jack said. "As soon as I'm approved for that mortgage we talked about." He had money tucked away for a down payment.

Bennett glanced at Leo. "About that…"

Jack turned to Leo, who was transfixed by a large aquarium inside. "Want to go look at the fish?"

"Sure." Leo scooted off his chair and darted toward the aquarium.

"That will keep him busy for a while." Jack placed his hands on the table. "You were saying?"

Bennett shook his head. "Based on the information you gave me, I couldn't find any lenders for you. When you're self-employed, it's difficult to qualify for a mortgage until you have a solid track record."

"Which I don't have yet." Jack could continue renting, but he wanted the dream of having his own home and the ability to do whatever he wanted with the property. And have something to pass on someday.

He wasn't getting any younger.

Garrett threaded his hands in front of him. "Why do you want to buy the place?"

"It's not for me," Jack replied. "I just got engaged, and I'd like to buy the house for her and my son."

"But you pay rent," Garrett said. "How do you manage that?"

Jack told him about his different jobs. The illustrations he was doing for Ginger, the articles, the royalties from other articles he'd kept the rights to, even how he was renting out the old studio space. He hated to mention his editor Gus, but if taking on that piece meant he might be able to buy the house, he'd do it.

When Jack finished, Bennett looked at the other man. "Jack is industrious, and he's at the top of his game. Plus, he has a substantial amount to put down on the property."

Garrett appeared to consider this and peered at Jack. "I understand you won a pretty impressive award in your profession."

Jack still felt self-conscious about that, although he'd

certainly put in the work for it. But so had a lot of his colleagues. "That I did."

"This is Jack's first marriage," Bennett added.

Jack grinned. "I just got formally engaged last night. If you can call Leo proposing over hot dogs on the beach formal."

"That's what I've always loved about Summer Beach." Garrett chuckled. "Tell me about this special lady."

Jack drew a breath. "Marina owns the Coral Cafe, a popular beachfront restaurant."

"Near the Coral Cottage?"

"Right on the same property."

"Then that would make her grandmother Ginger Delavie, yes?"

Jack often forgot how small Summer Beach really was. "How do you know Ginger?"

"Everyone knows Ginger. She's a force." Garrett laced his fingers. "If you're Ginger-approved, I see no reason why I shouldn't do the same."

"Sorry, I don't follow." Jack looked at Bennett, feeling a little lost in the conversation.

"I didn't think you'd be able to qualify for a loan right now," Bennett said, tapping the table. "And Garrett would have to do a lot of work to put the house on the market. If you want, he's agreed to carry the note for you—and at a very favorable interest rate. If that's okay with you, the house can be yours."

Worry fell from Jack's shoulders like weights. Just when he thought his day couldn't get any better, it did. "Wow, I hardly know what to say. Except thank you, and I promise I'll never be a day late." His bank's auto-pay was a lifesaver for his finances. "But I have to know—why would you take a chance on me?"

Garrett looked thoughtful. "People have paid it forward for

me." He nodded toward Leo. "Your boy reminds me of my kids at that age. I know what it's like to want to provide for your family. You have a home now, so take good care of Leo and Ginger's granddaughter. She must be an incredible woman."

"She sure is." Jack could hardly believe his good fortune. "And I'll do the same someday."

Bennett outlined the details. "If you both agree, Garrett's attorney can draw up the paperwork. Have yours look at it, too."

Just then, the food arrived, and Leo raced back to the table. Choked up with happiness, Jack wrapped his arms around his son. He'd tell Leo once the deal was signed off, although he wasn't sure Leo was old enough to appreciate the meaning of this. But someday, when his son had children, he would. And Jack would pay it forward, too. Tears sprang to his eyes. For the first time in his life, he could see his legacy unfolding before him.

"What's wrong, Dad?"

Jack laughed through his tears. "Sometimes, when your heart is so full of happiness, it leaks out of your eyes." He wiped his face while Bennett and Garrett looked on with understanding.

As they dug into the baskets lined with butcher paper and filled with steaming fried fish, french fries, and homemade tartar sauce, Jack thought food had never tasted so good.

Except for Marina's, of course. He couldn't wait to tell her. She'd once said that he should buy his rental when he could. He hoped she still felt that way.

As they were finishing the meal, Jack heard a young guy with his back to them at the bar take a phone call. As he spoke, the fine hairs on Jack's neck bristled with alarm.

It was the voice from the phone call at Marina's cafe. The guy who'd slipped away. And he was leaving now.

Jack leaned toward Bennett. "Would you look after Leo for a minute? I need to talk to someone."

Before Bennett could answer, Jack charged out the door after the other man, taking mental notes. Jeans, black T-shirt, short hair, muscled, tattoo on his neck.

There went his perfect day. Clenching his fists, Jack caught up with him in the dirt parking lot. "Hey bud, we need to talk."

The younger man whirled around. Designer sunglasses concealed his eyes. "What the—"

He stopped. "It's you." He took a step back and held up his hands. "I'm not looking for trouble."

"Then why are you spying on me?" The guy was younger than he'd thought. Not much more than a kid with a boarding school accent. This didn't add up.

"You've got that wrong."

"I don't think so. I heard your call at the Coral Cafe, right before you pulled a disappearing act." Jack advanced on him. "Who sent you?"

"Howling Cat Productions. But I was here anyway seeing friends."

That was not what Jack was expecting. He narrowed his eyes. "What do you want?"

"Look, my boss wanted me to track you down. We couldn't reach you in New York, and you'd left the newspaper. You're not even on social media."

"There's a reason for that. Once again, what do you want?"

"With Jarvis getting out of prison—"

"Hold it right there." Jack tapped the guy's chest. "If you're looking for trouble, I'm serving it up. Guaranteed."

The guy took another step back. "All we wanted was to talk to you about your investigation. For a film."

Jack shoved his hands on his hips. "Where are you from again?"

"Howling Cat Productions. It's in Hollywood."

"And you want to buy rights?"

"That's not really in the budget. We just want to talk to

you. Get a feel for what you think about the case. There's a famous director involved, and you could get some good press out of it. I could see if you can get some photos with him."

"Let me get this straight. There's no budget for me."

"They just what to pick your brain."

"For free?"

"Well, yeah. We have a team of screenwriters working on the script, but they're stuck, and we thought you might like to give us a fresh perspective. Can you jump on a call?"

"I'd like to tell them where to jump. As for you, stop nosing around and get out of here. I don't work for free. Not for Hollywood."

The guy spread his hands. "Look, I don't get paid either. It's a good way to break into the business." He backed toward his late-model Porsche.

Jack got it now. "You're an intern." Hollywood was famous for its unpaid, overworked interns looking for a break. Some were from wealthy families, while others were barely getting by.

"Not for long, I hope."

Swiping the air out of frustration, Jack expelled the pent-up adrenaline coursing through him. "Just get out here. And don't stalk people. Some folks aren't as nice as I am."

"My dad said you probably wouldn't go for it."

"You need to listen to your father more."

The kid stumbled back, clicked open his car, and climbed in, locking the door after him.

Jack turned away, disgusted. This wasn't the first time he'd received a request like that. A lot of people wanted shortcuts. They wanted to profit from others' work for nothing.

One of his colleagues had been in a lawsuit for years with a well-known director who'd effectively stolen his original screenplay, tweaked it, and made it into a blockbuster hit. The dirtbag had spent more on attorneys avoiding compensating his friend than if he'd simply bought the screenplay.

Jack was too old to play that game.

The kid gunned his fancy car and peeled out of the parking lot, leaving a cloud of dust. Jack coughed and started back to the restaurant.

But as he neared the door, an idea came to him, and he pulled out his phone. *Nothing ventured, nothing gained.* Would his luck hold out?

He tapped a quick message, then opened the door.

13

"We're being summoned," Marina said to Kai as they followed their grandmother into her spacious bedroom filled with antiques and mementos. Stepping into Ginger's room was like going through a portal in time.

Ginger led the way. "Since you're both engaged now, the timing is quite *apropos*," she said, her voice imperious as she led her granddaughters into her suite, where she'd lived for more than fifty years in between her world travels.

The sun shone into the bedroom, warming the honeyed wood floors worn smooth over the years. Ginger had placed soft, Persian silk rugs by the bed and in her sitting area away from the direct sunlight. A vintage chandelier sparkled overhead, and peach roses from the garden spilled from an antique crystal vase, perfuming the room. Silver-framed photos of Ginger and Bertrand with foreign dignitaries were carefully displayed.

Though the rest of the house was beach cottage chic, this room reflected Ginger's refined taste. The treasures in this room had been collected during her travels with Bertrand.

Kai turned to Marina and grinned. "Did you hear that old

Charlie at Java Beach is taking bets on whether you and Jack make it to the altar? That practically makes you a celebrity in Summer Beach."

"Already?" Though Marina supposed it was inevitable.

Ginger pursed her lips with disdain. "Charlie would take bets on the sunrise if he could find a willing fool."

"How are we stacking up to you and Axe?"

Kai quirked her mouth to one side. "Sorry to say, but you're considered a much longer shot. But you can still prove them wrong."

"Gee, thanks for the encouragement."

Marina was surprised that her engagement to Jack—and Leo—had zipped around Summer Beach in record time. She wondered who had unleashed the details, but then she recalled seeing a few locals on the beach not far from their party. The beach was a public gathering place, after all. And they hadn't exactly been quiet about Leo's proposal.

Ginger opened the door to her enormous custom closet. With a proud flourish, she brought out a zippered bag. "Heather helped me find this in the attic." She unzipped the fabric cover.

Marina leaned forward in anticipation.

"It's my wedding dress." Ginger withdrew a long, candle-light satin dress and draped it across the bed. "You may take it or leave it, of course. I wouldn't want to hinder your sense of style or self-expression."

Cherished memories rushed to Marina's mind.

Stroking the rich fabric with reverence, Ginger smiled. "This dress has been worn only two times. Once, when I married my dear Bertrand..." Her eyes lit with a faraway memory, and her words trailed off.

"Mom wore it, too," Marina added softly, lifting the hem.

"Yes. My darling Sandi." Ginger picked up a photo of their mother and father at their wedding on the beach. In the photo, she was wearing the dress. Next to that one was a black-and-white wedding photo of Ginger and Bertrand. "Your mother looked like an angel in this dress. It carries with it so many happy memories."

"For me, too." Marina ran her hand over the shimmering fabric, admiring it anew. Through windows facing the ocean, the sun cast a glow across the dress. Marina's heart filled with an old longing. "I remember the day I begged Mom to put on this dress. I told her she looked like a fairy princess, and she promised that one day I would wear it, too. For my wedding."

That scene had filled Marina's thoughts for years, and she'd always assumed she would wear this exquisite gown. But now, as the gorgeous vintage dress called to her, other memories flooded back.

When she'd married Stan, they'd been in such a rush before he was to ship out that they'd opted for a simple ceremony with the chaplain. There hadn't been time for her grandmother to mail the dress across the country—or even time to make the wedding—so she'd hastily bought an outfit from a local boutique.

Marina could hardly believe she was getting married again. Thanks to Leo, she was getting a second chance with the man she loved. She smiled at the memory of Jack's awkward proposal following Leo's. Surely, they'd laugh about it all someday.

The rest of the town already was.

"Why haven't I ever seen this dress?" Kai asked, a trace of sadness edging her words.

"You were pretty young at the time," Marina replied.

Kai frowned. "I don't remember Brooke wearing it."

"That's right," Ginger said. "She wore a cotton lace dress with her Birkenstocks under it. Comfort first is dear Brooke's motto. She looked lovely, too."

Lifting the dress with care, Marina held it to her shoulders, and it puddled beautifully on the floor, even though she stood on her tiptoes. Kai had Ginger's height, while she and

Brooke were shorter. She glanced in the mirror at her reflection. The soft, candlelight shade brought out her new hair color.

Kai's lower lip extended in a little pout that Marina instantly recognized. "It's so pretty."

Marina had always felt sorry for her sister, who had been so young when their parents had been taken from them. Marina had been preparing to go to college, and Brooke was just starting high school, so they were both old enough to have vivid memories of their parents. Not so with Kai.

"I'm sure Sandi would have loved for any of her girls to wear it." A smile wreathed Ginger's face as she gazed diplomatically between them. "It was certainly one of the happiest days of my life."

Eyeing the dress, Kai put a hand on her hip and frowned. "It's too long for you, Marina."

"I can hem it."

"But I wouldn't need to. Let me try it on."

"But I—" Before Marina could finish, Kai peeled off her sundress and reached for the wedding gown. With a gulp, Marina relinquished it to her.

Her sister slithered into a cascade of rippling fabric. The bias-cut satin skimmed her narrow hips and clung to her figure in all the right places. Kai twirled in front of the mirror. With Kai's hair, she looked like an ivory goddess from head to toe.

"See? It's perfect for me."

So it is, Marina thought, self-consciously straightening as she tightened her stomach muscles. Spending her days in the kitchen tasting dishes she created had added a little extra girth to her frame. When she'd been a news anchor in San Francisco, she'd had to keep her weight in check. Yet, after losing that job and moving to Summer Beach, she'd found freedom in not having to watch every bite.

Marina felt Ginger's gaze on her as if waiting for her

approval. A sinking feeling hollowed her chest. How could she deny her younger sister this dream?

Squelching her desire, Marina put her arm around Kai's slender shoulders and peered at her sister in the mirror. "This dress looks like it was made for you. So, it's yours to wear."

Kai flung her arms around Marina. "You're the best. I was afraid you'd be upset."

"Me?" Marina managed a strangled laugh. "Oh, I have something else in mind." Over her sister's shoulder, she saw Ginger nod her approval.

Inside, Marina's heart was crushed as her dream withered away. Yet, this was the right thing to do, she told herself. The dress looked better on Kai. Her sister spent her days practicing dance routines and performing. She had Ginger's lean physique, too. Besides, this was Kai's first wedding.

Still, Marina wanted to look her best for Jack. This was her forever wedding—the fates willing, that is. She bit her lip.

"You'll both be beautiful brides." Embracing Marina and Kai, Ginger kissed each of them on the cheek. "Your mother is surely smiling down on you now."

And Ginger had lost her only daughter, Marina reminded herself, feeling small for begrudging Kai the opportunity of feeling close to the mother she'd barely known. To have another chance to marry a man she truly loved was something Marina had hardly dared to imagine.

Surely that was enough for her.

Kai stepped out of the dress. "I'm glad that's settled. Axe and I still have a lot of work to do on the new show. If you don't mind, I'll take this with me. See you later."

As soon as Kai left, Ginger reached into another garment bag. "Since Kai is wearing the wedding gown, I thought you might like this." She brought out a long swath of vintage lace.

"This is the sheer coat I wore over the dress. It was just enough on a balmy summer evening. And it's easy to hem. Your mother wore this, too." She nodded to a smaller photo.

"It's so pretty," Marina said, her spirits guarded. "But if it goes with the dress, shouldn't Kai wear this, too?"

"It's probably too conservative for Kai's taste, don't you think?" A smile danced on Ginger's face. She held the garment up to Marina's shoulders. "This sheer lace coat will be spectacular over a simple sheath. My dear Bertrand called it the epitome of elegance. Years later, I wore it again to a ball in Paris with all the important diplomats. This is quite a special piece."

Marina embraced her grandmother. "You always know just what to say."

"Well, it was better than dividing the dress." Ginger gave a soft laugh. "But you were admirably magnanimous. A sure mark of character."

Marina's cheeks flamed with embarrassment. "Actually, I was struggling over that."

"That was clear to see. Well, clear to me, dear. Not to Kai, of course." Ginger patted Marina's hand. "Jack will love seeing you in this." Leveling her gaze at Marina, she asked, "He's still committed?"

Marina nodded with a high degree of certainty. "He wants another do-over at Beaches."

"Maybe that handsome new pediatrician helped spur him to action."

AFTER THE BUSY lunch run at the cafe, Marina left her new cook Cruise in charge of the kitchen. The food truck was being delivered today. When she saw Judith pull the vehicle to the side of the road in front of the cafe, Marina went out to greet her.

"Here she is," Judith called out from the window. She stepped out with a sheaf of papers. "I got Bessie all cleaned up for you, and if you're happy, we can sign all the final paperwork. Have a look inside."

Marina stepped into the truck. Immediately, she could see that Judith had taken extra care in cleaning it. She saw stacks of paper napkins and other supplies in the cabinets. "Do you want these supplies?"

"I have no use for them, so they're yours if you want them."

"I sure do, thanks. I plan to take her out this weekend. My sister is having a show at the Seashell."

"I heard the holiday show last year was pretty funny. I wish I'd seen that." Judith leaned against the vehicle. "I've called her Bessie, but you can give her a new name."

Marina paused. "I've been thinking about Coralina. It will go well with her new paint job."

"I'm so glad you're taking over. I'm excited to leave and start my new life in New Zealand, but it makes me happy to know that Bessie—Coralina, that is—will be in good hands with you. It took me a long time to get everything just the way I wanted in her."

"I can see all the little details you've added. And the flowers are beautiful. How thoughtful." A small vase filled with roses was attached to a wall. Judith had thought of everything.

The other woman demonstrated how everything worked. "The vase is on a swinging arm, so you can push it out of the serving window when you're parked and open for business. Flowers give good vibes. People used to comment on this all the time."

"I'll bet they did." Marina could just imagine how coral roses from Ginger's garden would look in it and subtly convey her brand. Often, it was the little touches that welcomed people and made them feel at home.

Heather hurried across the patio. "Hey, Mom. Is this the new addition?"

Marina introduced her daughter and Judith. "Meet

Coralina. Her maiden voyage will be opening night of the new show."

A thoughtful look filled Heather's face. "Wow, we can have some fun with this. I know a lot of concerts that Cruise and I could take this to. Or just up and down the beach on the weekends." She began to explore inside.

"Looks like we have a deal." Marina handed Judith the cashier's check from her bank, and the two women signed the documents and shook hands.

When they stepped from the vehicle, Judith handed Marina the keys. "I hope you'll have many adventures in this food truck."

"And I wish you the very best for your wedding and the new restaurant." Marina gave her a hug.

"Unexpected new chapters of life are a lot of fun," Judith said.

Marina jingled the keys with happiness. "That's what my grandmother says."

She'd tried to do everything to get ready for her next chapters. The food truck was here and ready to go. As for the Jack chapter, she wished she could be as certain. Once stood up, twice shy.

14

"Welcome to Kai's Broadway bridal shower." Marina waved a group of women into the Coral Cafe.

Billie, Jen, and Leilani had done a marvelous job of decorating in such a short time, but then they'd also raided the costume and prop storage at the theater. Many were already in costume.

"Right this way," Heather said. She wore a jaunty little usher's cap over her long hair.

"The hat looks better on you," Marina said. Hers kept slipping off.

"I have bobby pins that hold it on. You can have a couple." Heather dipped her mother's cap to the side and pinned it. "And it looks better at an angle."

Marina glanced at her reflection in a window. The theater usher costume consisted of a red jacket with black slacks. It was fun to dress up, and it put everyone in a party mood. "Much better, thanks. Kai will make you wardrobe master in no time."

Straightening her jacket, Heather laughed. "No thanks. I have enough work."

"Ethan mentioned you have a new internship."

"He wasn't supposed to say anything yet." With a happy, secretive look, Heather added, "It's not even final, but I'll tell you later. Here, take some programs."

Marina began passing out programs in the style of the iconic *Playbill* often distributed in theaters. *Kai's Broadway Bridal Shower* was printed on the front. Inside was the menu and a list of performers. Heather had used her graphic skills to create and print the program just this morning.

Marina had planned the late lunch as a buffet with chilled shrimp cocktails, avocado toast points, and street tacos with mango salsa. Cold avocado gazpacho and a salad bar rounded out the light, easy fare.

On such short notice, Ginger and Brooke had pitched in to help prepare the luncheon, and Marina had brought in her new extra staff. They'd done a lot of the prep work in Ginger's kitchen during the lunch run at the cafe. The food was ready just in time, but just barely. Still, that was half the fun, Ginger insisted.

Ivy and Shelly were among the first to arrive, along with several of Kai's theater friends—women and men—from Los Angeles.

"Wow, how fancy," Shelly said, gazing around.

Props and mementos from the theater were placed around the patio. Painted scene pieces of shopfronts, giant gift boxes, and a faux palm tree decorated with beach ornaments made up the eclectic decorations.

"And just look at the tables," Ivy added.

On every table were flowers from Blossoms flower stand. Imani, the proprietor, had arrived early to arrange the flowers. Ginger had contributed her vintage crystal, silver, and china place settings. They had mixed patterns for a festive cottage look. Leilani had placed buckets of flowering plants on the patio, creating a lush oasis.

On another table, guests had piled up gifts. Kai didn't

have much more than clothes to take to Axe's bungalow because she'd been living out of suitcases for years. Still, Ginger had a few things set aside for her.

Axe's small home near the village was well-maintained, though he'd invested his money in building his construction business, along with his other dream, the amphitheater.

Wearing a short, Hawaiian floral-print dress and a flower lei, Kai hurried toward the group, her arms held wide. "I'm so glad you all made it," she exclaimed amidst a flurry of air kisses and hugs. She clasped hands with a new arrival, a twenty-something version of herself, a slender women with a similar mane of blond hair. "Especially you, Madison. You were the best understudy I ever had."

The younger woman beamed. "When you left so suddenly, I got my shot at your part, so I'll always be grateful to you for that."

"It was time to bow out and start a new chapter," Kai said happily.

Marina knew it hadn't been quite that seamless of a professional exit for her sister, but this was no time to bring up Kai's ex, Dmitri. Madison had been thoughtful about that. And Kai seemed unbothered by that now.

"Now you can meet everyone." Kai waved across the cafe, which Marina had closed after the lunch crowd for the party. "Billie, look who just drove in."

Her friends exchanged hugs, and laughter swept through the throng of people. Madison had driven with several others from the cast that Kai had been a part of. They'd performed and traveled together for years.

"We want to meet Axe," Madison said eagerly. "Only you would meet a singing Montana cowboy on the beach."

Billie arched an eyebrow. "He's hot, too."

"You'll get your chance." Kai grinned as she flung her arms around her friends. "We'll all meet at Spirits & Vine after the party. He might have a couple friends with him, too."

"Single?"

"Many are." Kai winked. "And you must all stay for our opening night at the Seashell. It's the world premiere of our *Belles on the Beach.*"

"We wouldn't miss it," Madison said. "We're all piling into rooms at the Seabreeze Inn."

They went on to talk about other mutual friends. Most everyone in this crowd had known Dmitri, the man Kai had been engaged to before. Marina was glad no one mentioned the New York producer. She couldn't imagine how Kai might have ever been happy with him.

Axe, on the other hand, was a generous, warm-hearted man who shared Kai's love of performing. Hearing them sing duets on a starry night at the Seashell was magical. They had truly found their calling—and found each other.

Marina enjoyed chatting with Kai's friends who had performed Broadway hits across the country. They were all as different as they could be, but every one of them was a talented, hard-working actor. Soon, they were all talking and laughing.

A few minutes later, Marina tapped a glass with a spoon to get everyone's attention. "We have appetizers and drinks available for anyone who's parched and hungry."

"That would be me," Madison said. "But Kai, you have to go first."

As the women fell in line at the buffet table, Ginger made her entrance from the cottage. She wore a long floral hostess dress with layered strands of turquoise necklaces.

Kai proudly tucked her arm through Ginger's. "You've all heard me talk about my grandmother. This is the fabulous Ginger Delavie, to whom my sisters and I owe everything."

Ginger kissed Kai's cheek. "My dear, you would have done it on your own—with or without me. You're the indomitable trio."

"Where do you think we got that from?" Brooke asked.

Marina laughed with her. The three of them had followed different paths and had different styles, but here they were, reunited at last.

Soon all the guests had filled their plates and sat down to eat under the coral umbrellas. Marina was pleased that Kai's guests enjoyed the food.

When they had finished eating, Billie tapped her glass for attention. "For Kai's bridal shower, Broadway has come to Summer Beach. Since we're all sisters here, let's kick this off with a number from *Hamilton!*"

Cheers went up, and at that, three women dressed in period costumes emerged from the rear of the cottage where Marina had set up dressing rooms in Ginger's den and Bertrand's old library, which still held the faint aroma of his vanilla pipe tobacco.

One of Kai's friends had arranged the music, and he cranked up a tune. The trio burst into song, belting out their version of "Helpless."

Cheers went up from the crowd, and soon people were singing along. Next, one of the couples from Los Angeles took their places and sang a love song from *West Side Story,* "Somewhere (There's A Place For Us)."

Then, more friends spilled out with other songs until everyone was on their feet, clapping for Kai until she joined them in the last song. It was from *The Lion King,* "Can You Feel the Love Tonight?" Soon, they were all swaying in song.

Marina loved seeing Kai in her element. "She's incredibly talented," she said to Ginger and Brooke. She was also eager to see the new production Kai and Axe had been working on. "She's really coming into her own now with her writing and directing."

Ginger smiled and pressed her palms together. "Kai is a treasure, but each one of you is just as talented in your chosen specialty." She beamed at them. "My three wonderful grand-daughters."

"Don't forget the next generation," Brooke said. "Looks like Oakley has his great-grandmother's aptitude for math."

"Indeed he does," Ginger said, pride evident in her voice. "You've done a fine job of encouraging him. I'll bet he'd be fascinated with codes and ciphers. Why, I should teach all of them, including the upcoming addition to the family, young Leo." She smiled at Marina. "What maturity he has."

Marina knew the reason for that. Vanessa was a wonderful mother, but having to endure her illness and meeting the father he had never known had given Leo a level of maturity beyond his years. Maybe that's why he'd had the foresight to read his father's mind and propose to her. And perhaps that proposal wasn't as impetuous as it seemed.

More than anything, Marina wanted Leo to enjoy being a carefree little boy. Most days, running on the beach with Scout was all he needed to bring a smile to his face, yet Marina resolved to be the best stepmother he could want.

When the entertainment concluded, Marina excused herself to check on the food. Kai hooked her arm in Marina's and went with her. "This party is wonderful, and it means the world to me. Thank you for turning all this out on such short notice."

"I had a lot of help, but for you, anything," Marina said. And she meant it. She wanted Kai to go into her marriage in the happiest frame of mind.

Kai followed her into the kitchen. "What are we going to do for your bridal shower?"

Marina brought out a dessert tray of chocolate mousse in miniature glasses and a bowl of whipped cream she'd prepared earlier. "Now that I'm officially engaged to Jack and Leo?"

"Leo is adorable," Kai said. "Oh, my gosh, if he'd asked me, I think I would say yes, too. Axe would have been so disappointed, but how could anyone say no to that little man?"

Marina shook her head, still marveling at the boy's actions. "Actually, what I said was *yeesy Louisey*, but that was good enough for Leo."

"And Jack, evidently," Kai added, smiling. "So, should we plan a shower for you soon?"

"I don't need one, but it's nice of you to think about it. Jack and I have everything we need." As they spoke, Marina spooned whipped cream onto the chocolate mousse dessert cups.

Kai perched on a stool beside the kitchen counter. "Any mention of a ring yet?"

"A simple band will do. I have my hands in all sorts of food all day long, remember?" That's what she'd worn with Stan, and she'd been happy with that.

Kai's face fell. "I'm sure he's going to do something else for you."

"We're in a different place than you and Axe. We have children to think of first."

At that, Kai's eyes widened. "Are you thinking of having more?"

Marina nudged her. "Bite your tongue."

"What? All I'm saying is, it's still possible, right?"

"Technically, I suppose. But no. We're done."

Kai's eyes twinkled, and she picked up a dessert. "We'll see about that."

Marina was eager to change the subject. "And you and Axe?"

"That's going to be a surprise." Kai picked up a spoon and dug into the creamy chocolate. "Oh, this is fabulous."

Marina plopped a dollop of whipped cream on the small glass. "Like your wedding date? People need to know when it is so they can plan. There's not much time left this summer."

Kai smiled impishly, ignoring her as she scooped out the chocolate and cream. "Yum, this is delicious."

"The date, Kai. You were the one who wanted to move

everything up." Marina frowned while her sister continued to avoid the question. "Has something happened?"

Kai finished the dessert with one big spoonful and put the glass down. "I'm not worried. I'm sure everyone will be there."

That made no sense to Marina. "Are you planning some sort of flash mob wedding on Main Street? Or at the beach?"

Kai snapped her fingers. "Not a bad idea…" With a mysterious smile, she swung around and made her way back to her guests.

By the time the party had moved to Spirits & Vine on Main Street, everyone was having a wonderful time. Marina stepped inside the busy wine bar and followed Kai to where Axe had already staked out a section for them.

She'd already changed from the usher costume she'd worn at Kai's shower. That had been a fun outfit, though a little warm in the summer sun. The bright yellow dress she'd paired with multi-colored wedges lifted her spirits even more. From cooking for loved ones to chatting with friends and family, it had been a nearly perfect day.

"Marina, over here." Jack waved from the long end of a table, where he sat with a glass of red wine and a charcuterie board in front of him.

"I didn't know you'd be here." She was delighted to see him.

He gave her a soft kiss. "Thought I might surprise you. In a good way, this time. I think I'm going to be apologizing for standing you up at dinner for a long time."

She twined her fingers with his. "The barbecue the other night was a good start."

"Ah, Leo, what a kid. I promise I didn't put him up to that. I'm not that smart." He drew his brow in concern. "Are you sure you don't want to reconsider? I know I'm not the best prize, and I heard about the new doctor giving you a lift home."

Her senses prickled around her neck, and she sighed. Was his old habit of avoidance returning? "What if I decide not to let you out of that promise?"

Relief flooded his face. "You really mean it?"

"I wouldn't have said *yes* if I didn't mean it."

"Well, now that you mention it, who's Louise?"

At the next table, the owner of the Laundry Basket looked up, and Jack put up his hands. "Sorry, I didn't mean you, Louise."

"You're impossible." Marina jabbed him playfully in the ribs. "I'm giving you thirty seconds to put a glass of wine in front of me, or I'm moving on. Even if you are the best-looking guy here." Marina folded her arms and let her gaze trail over him. What he did to a white knit shirt shouldn't be allowed. Jack wasn't only running on the beach; he looked like he'd been lifting something much heavier than a sketch pencil or a keyboard.

Jack quickly pushed his glass toward her and signaled the waiter. "The bridal shower must have been a tough tour of duty."

Marina chuckled and leaned toward him. If they could keep laughing through mishaps, they'd have a chance. Life was never smooth.

Jack swept his arm around her and gave her a light, feathery kiss. "I'll do my best not to let you down. I can't say I won't because life gets in the way sometimes, but I'll try every day." He went on, nuzzling her neck. "I love you, Marina. More than I ever thought possible. I'm the luckiest guy in the world."

These were the words she loved to hear. But before she could respond, Kai and her friends joined them at the table, and the party continued.

A little later, after finishing their wine and the charcuterie board, Jack took her hand. "I was going to wait, but I have something I want to share with you sooner rather than later. Will you come back to the house with me?"

Marina agreed, curious as to what it might be. They walked back to Jack's cottage by the sea. As they approached the front porch, heavy metal music blasted behind the house.

"Someone's having a party." Marina nodded toward a police cruiser that had just turned onto the street. "It almost sounds like it's coming from your place."

Jack scrubbed his chin. "Probably my short-term tenants in the studio. They'll be gone soon, but they've been a problem."

"Do you have to rent out that unit?"

"It helps. I'd better tell them to turn down the music. A neighbor probably called the police again."

"Bet that's making you popular."

Marina could feel the base throbbing. So could the neighbors, she imagined. The cruiser stopped in front of the house, and the imposing form of Chief Clarkson stepped from the vehicle.

"I can guess why you're here." Jack looked sheepish. "I've been away, but I'll tell the guys to turn down the music."

"We can't make this a habit," Clark said. "Your neighbors deserve better."

"They're just a bunch of guys here to surf and have a good time. I didn't think this would be a problem, but I'll tell them right now."

"This time, I'll go with you." The chief hitched up his belt full of gear.

Jack opened the door, and they walked through the bungalow. Scout was whimpering in a corner of the kitchen, and Marina knelt to console him.

"Poor baby, that music is too loud for you, isn't it?" She'd talked Jack into installing a doggie door in the kitchen for Scout. Even the dog needed some peace and quiet.

She wondered how long Jack would want to rent the rear studio. While she could appreciate the extra income, she preferred having privacy. Especially if the guests were all of this ilk.

While Jack and the chief continued through to the rear yard, Marina turned to look for a treat in the kitchen for Scout. She shoved aside empty cereal boxes and dirty dishes.

"Look at this mess," she muttered.

Besides the kitchen disaster, Jack looked like he'd been working in the kitchen for some reason. His laptop computer and drawing material were strewn across the kitchen table. The curtains were drawn.

Scout whimpered as if in guilty agreement.

"Not you, boy." Gingerly, she shoved aside a stack of old pizza boxes. Now she knew what Jack ate when he wasn't at the cafe.

Dirty dishes filled the sink, too. From the looks of it, he'd been making eggs. And pancakes. She wrinkled her nose. The stovetop, the oven, the refrigerator—all of it needed a good cleaning. And the floor.

She'd been so busy that she hadn't been here in some time. A box of dog treats sat next to a macaroni-and-cheese mix. She pulled out a crunchy bone and gave it to Scout, who gobbled it up in one bite.

With Jack still outside, Marina walked through the house, wondering if the rest of it was a mess, too.

The living room wasn't too bad. Just stacks of books and mail, although most of it hadn't been opened, even bills, which struck her as careless. Jack's room had dirty laundry everywhere, and the small black-and-white hexagonal tiles in the bathrooms needed a good scrubbing. A mound of damp towels lay in the corner. She wrinkled her nose at the sour odor.

She peeked into Leo's room, which wouldn't win any

awards for cleanliness either, but he was still a child. There was a pathway to his bed through the toys and dirty clothes.

With some dismay, she realized this was how Jack really lived. Not that she was a neat freak, and she certainly hadn't thought he was, but his habits were far worse than she'd thought.

Jack clearly didn't understand the basics of picking up after himself—or teaching his son to do that. He must have stashed the mess when she'd been over before, but most of the time he went to the cafe or met her at her house.

As Marina walked back into the living room, her gaze fell on a torn shipping box on the table by the stack of mail. A faded, red velvet jewelry container sat next to it. Intrigued, she walked toward it and rested her fingers lightly on what looked like a vintage ring box. She was dying to open it.

Maybe this is why he'd brought her back here.

The loud, thumping music suddenly ceased. Glancing around to make sure she was still alone, Marina surveyed the overall state of the house, and her heart fell.

An alarm of warning clanged in her mind.

She drew her hand back as sharply as she'd snatched it from the fire the other night. The scope of responsibility that would rest on her shoulders dawned on her.

At once, the memory of all the years of cleaning up after her children came rushing back. She'd taught Heather and Ethan to care for their home, even though their apartment overlooking the San Francisco Bay had been smaller than this. It hadn't been easy, but they'd managed.

When the twins left for college, her workload had plummeted. The apartment was too quiet then, but she didn't miss falling into bed at midnight after doing laundry for school the next day. Not when she had to rise by four to make it to the studio for the morning broadcast. Makeup, concealer, and coffee had figured prominently in her daily arsenal for years.

Just thinking about those hardships quickened her breath.

Was this a chapter she wanted to reopen? Of course, there had been joy as well, but she'd worked so hard for so many years that running a cafe seemed fun and easy in comparison.

And this situation was worse. Jack was a grown man who appeared to have no inclination to lift a finger. Who'd never stayed in one place long enough to call it home or care for it, she realized. No doubt, it would be up to her to oversee everything. Is this how she wanted to spend the rest of her life?

Scout trotted to her and sat on her feet, looking up with expectation.

Marina reached down to stroke his snout. "And I bet you're hungry."

He brushed his head against her legs as if she'd understood his need. She rubbed Scout's neck, feeling bad for the poor pup. The memory of the tacos drenched in hot sauce came to mind as well.

Maybe she'd been blinded by Jack's professional accomplishments and smooth words. By comparison, Stan had been in the military; he made a neater bed than she did.

Marina backed away from the table just as Jack and Clark came through the kitchen doorway.

"I'll be on my way," the chief said as he made his way toward the front door. "Good to see you, Marina."

"Likewise, Clark."

Jack shut the door behind him. "I don't think we'll have any more trouble with those guys tonight." His gaze darted to the ring box on the table. "We can sit on the couch, and I'll open the windows for a view of the ocean. Would you like another glass of wine?"

Marina pressed her lips together. Being in love with Jack and actually living with Jack might be two very different things. She'd come so far in creating the life she wanted in Summer Beach. Was she ready to walk away and spend the rest of it picking up the dirty socks of a careless slob?

As bright as Jack might be, she had her standards. Ginger's advice floated to mind.

"I should go." Leaving Jack with his mouth agape, she turned toward the door and hurried down the porch steps. She realized she was much like her grandmother after all.

Standards, and all that.

While Marina fled into the night toward her home, she could hear the music cranking up again.

a s the sun was setting, Marina maneuvered her bright yellow food truck into the Seashell, the amphitheater that backed up to the cliff on one side and opened to an ocean view on the other. Heather and Brooke sat in the front of the cab with her, and in the back were boxed picnic dinners that patrons had ordered.

Tonight was the opening night for *Belles on the Beach*. Kai even had official colors for the night; she'd asked everyone to wear pink or white, saying they could dress up as much as they liked. Marina and Heather wore pink sundresses, and Brooke paired a rose-colored shirt with white jeans and Birkenstock sandals.

Even the sky has orchestrated her sunset at Kai's behest with mauve ribbons flung across the heavens.

"I'm so excited for Kai and Axe," Heather said. "I hope they get good reviews for this show. They must have felt a lot of pressure to top the holiday production."

"I understand how they feel." Marina had jittery nerves, too. "This is Coralina's opening night."

"Do you hear that?" Heather patted the vehicle's dashboard. "We're counting on you, Coralina."

"Who names a food truck?" Brooke asked. "Or talks to one?"

"I can't believe you said that," Marina replied, laughing. "You know the Delavie-Moore family doesn't do anything ordinary—yourself included."

"I'll say." Brooke laughed and did a little drumbeat on the dash. "Let's go, Coralina. It's showtime for you."

"How many picnic boxes did we end up with for tonight?" Marina asked.

Heather named a number and added, "We're definitely up by a few orders each time."

Marina nodded thoughtfully. "As much as we promote the box meals, relatively few people who attend actually plan ahead to order them."

"Especially tourists who buy tickets the day of the performance," Brooke said. "You've put a lot into this food truck. It's bound to explode your business."

"That's the plan." Marina slowed the truck. "And I hope *Belles on the Beach* will be another hit for Kai and Axe. They put so much effort into the production."

Heather peered ahead. "That looks like a good spot to park right there, Mom. People can't miss this banana-yellow truck."

"Which will soon be bright coral."

Next week, her food truck would go in for painting, but Marina didn't want to miss an opportunity—and she wanted to have a practice run with a friendly audience tonight. Since this was opening night, Kai and Axe had given complimentary tickets to all their family and close friends in Summer Beach. Kai's friends had all stayed for the performance.

Marina leaned from the driver's window and waved at Kai, who was talking to the stage manager and volunteer ushers. She wore black leggings and a T-shirt. In her hands, she held a stack of programs, and she was passing them out.

"Where shall I park?" Marina called out.

Kai excused herself and made her way toward them, pointing out a spot alongside the seating area. "Right there will be perfect. When people line up, they won't be in the walkway. And we've reserved seats in the front for all of you. That's where family is, so be sure to sit there."

"We'll join everyone before curtain time," Marina said. Tonight was a real family effort. Heather and Brooke had put in a lot of time boxing the dinners, including special orders for gluten-free, diabetic, and vegetarian options, and preparing the food truck for the day.

Ginger had come up with the idea of having a large Coral Cafe banner printed to put over the existing submarine sandwich logo on the vehicle. She'd picked it up at the printer, and they'd affixed it to the truck right before they left. It was good enough for the trial run.

Marina parked, and they got out. It was then that she noticed bouquets of roses and lilies trimming the section in the front. "Looks like you're going all out tonight."

"It's opening night, and it's a show about weddings, so I thought, why not?" Kai laughed, and her voice sounded a little high-pitched. She had a pencil poking through her haphazard bun.

Instantly, Marina recognized the nervous laughter but decided it was only Kai's opening night jitters. She wondered why she and Axe had chosen Saturday instead of a slower night to debut, but that wasn't any of her business.

Brooke motioned toward the programs. "I'd love to see one."

"Sure." Kai passed them out, her hand shaking slightly as she did.

Kai should be used to opening night performances, Marina thought. She was a true professional, after all.

Brooke opened the program. "Look at this. Written and directed by Kai Moore. I'm so proud of you." She hugged her sister.

That explained it, Marina thought. This time, Kai was also the scriptwriter and director. In the past, even if a show didn't get great reviews, Kai usually did for her performance. This time, however, the responsibility was all hers. "Break a leg, Kai."

That was theater language for wishing someone good luck, but no one dared to actually say that, as that was thought to attract supreme bad luck.

Heather read the introduction. "Three sisters with wedding aspirations wreak havoc in a beach town."

Brooke put a finger to her temple. "Three sisters? I wonder where you got that."

"Inspiration only," Kai said, sticking another pencil into her bun. "This is a series of wedding comedies, sort of like *My Big Fat Greek Wedding*. Remember when I had a part in that? Live audiences always love wedding disasters." She paused, glancing at Marina. "Not that yours will be like that."

If at all. Marina had exchanged a few rushed texts with Jack this morning. She didn't know how to broach the subject of his disastrous living environment without insulting him. Or worse, mothering him. But the way he was living was an insult. To Leo and Scout, and certainly to Jack, too.

After seeing the state of his house, her rational side had taken the reins. She refused to be a mother to a grown man. But she couldn't think about that tonight. She had an important job ahead of her.

They all did.

"I have to get in makeup and costume, but I know you'll be fabulous." Kai's face was flushed and her smile wavered. "It's going to be spectacular, right?"

"Of course," Marina replied. "You've got this."

As she watched Kai dash off, she wondered if her sister had reason to be nervous. Perhaps the stage play script wasn't as strong as she would have liked. Or maybe she was having problems with the cast.

If so, it was even more important that they were all here, Marina decided. They would support Kai no matter what.

Marina opened the rear door to the food truck. "Time to set up."

"Tell us what you need," Brooke said.

"Would you open the serving window and put out snack items, napkins, straws, plastic cutlery—all the things people ask for? Heather, would you put on fresh coffee, just in case, and set out the menu board? I'll get my food production line organized. Let's offer samples, too."

"I'll make a tray of brownies and chocolate chip cookie bits." Brooke reached for a plate. "Those are popular at the farmers market."

Marina liked that idea. "Then let's put the cookies on display by the register."

"I'll plug in the lights before we get busy." Heather turned on a string of lights she'd brought to bring attention to the vehicle.

"Wow." Marina stepped back. The lights were a good idea. "Can't miss this. We'll have to turn off the lights during the show."

Before long, audience members began arriving. Heather and Brooke divided the work, with one line for the box dinner pickup and another for new food orders. The brownies and cookies were going fast.

Marina had put a chef jacket over her sundress, and she focused on assembling orders from the fairly easy menu she'd created. Cheese and charcuterie boards, chopped salad, and toasted nuts had been pre-made in her cafe kitchen. Here in the food truck, she made sweet potato fries with garlic aioli and mile-high deli sandwiches. Since they had a mobile liquor license, they also offered small splits of wine and champagne that were easy to manage.

Even Ginger joined them, chatting up the line, making suggestions, and offering samples. She was their ambassador, and they needed that. So many people knew Ginger, and if the line moved a little slower than it should, folks didn't mind if they were talking to her.

Marina grinned at her grandmother. A secret diplomatic weapon, indeed.

As Marina worked, Heather leaned back. "We're taking orders for intermission, too. People are asking for that because they're accustomed to it at other theaters. We could add that to our website later. Maybe have an app for that."

"Brilliant ideas," Marina said, juggling the fries and sandwiches.

When a bell rang signaling the curtain time in a few minutes, they quickly cleared the line and served the last orders. Marina, Heather, and Brooke traded exuberant high-fives.

Ginger applauded their efforts. "Well done, ladies. I'd say Coralina is off to a smashing success."

Marina could see Kai peeking out at the crowd, and she waved at her. "I'm sure the show will be, too."

Marina sealed the food truck window and turned off the lights. They took their places with the rest of the group in the seats Kai had reserved for them. Marina sat on the end.

Brooke's husband, Chip, was there with their three boys, and Ethan was sitting with them. He was devouring one of Marina's pastrami sandwiches with sweet potato fries and coleslaw.

Ethan took the last bite. "That was really good, Mom."

"Glad you liked it." Marina felt a deep sense of satisfaction. She hadn't tallied the income yet, but based on how many items they'd sold, her food truck idea was going to pay off.

Marina looked around. All of Kai's friends were seated together, too. Jen and George, Leilani and Roy, and Shelly and Ivy with Bennett and Mitch. Her theater friends, including Billie and Madison, were together, too.

Marina heard a small voice beside her, and she turned.

"Can we sit with you?" Leo asked. He held his father's hand.

"Of course." She scooted over. How could she say no to Leo? As for Jack, well, that remained to be seen.

Nothing wrong with just enjoying each other's company, Ginger had repeated. *I have wintered into this wisdom*, she'd added, paraphrasing *Beowulf.* That's what Marina would do for now. At this stage of life, not everyone needed marriage.

After all, Ginger had her Bertrand, and Marina had her Stan, if only for the briefest time.

The stars were coming out as the stage lights went up. In the first scene, Kai made her entrance with other cast members to a wave of applause.

As the show got underway, Marina marveled at how Kai's talent was growing. She'd evolved from a pure performer into a writer and director with a unique vision. If she had stayed with the touring theater company, she would never have had the opportunity to stretch in her profession like this.

Kai's comedic timing was excellent, and the audience roared with laughter at the stories of the three women known as the belles and their hysterical wedding dilemmas.

Just before intermission, Marina excused herself and hurried back to the food truck with Brooke and Heather. Business was brisk, and she was relieved and happy. Buying this truck had been a good decision.

Intermission became a mad scramble for patrons to pick up their orders and buy other items. Marina didn't have time to cook much, but they had plenty of snacks. When the stage lights flickered, everyone hurried to their seats. Marina made her way through the crowd with Brooke and Heather.

Billie stopped Marina on the way. "Kai sent me. She needs the three of you to join her backstage. And Ginger and Ethan, too." She named a precise time.

"Does Kai need extras?"

"Something like that," Billie replied. "Be sure to meet me at the stage door on the side. And don't be late."

Acting on stage wasn't Marina's favorite pastime, but she could stand in a crowd scene. And she knew Heather and Ginger would enjoy it. She looked at Brooke and Heather, who both nodded. "We'll be there."

When Marina sat down, she noticed the rest of Kai's friends had disappeared. She assumed it must be a scene that needed a lot of extras. She took her seat and told Ginger, who also agreed to join Kai.

The second half was even more entertaining than the first, with Kai and Axe taking the lead roles as an engaged couple plagued with one catastrophe after the next. The question was: Would they make it to the altar?

A little while later, Marina's phone vibrated on silent mode. It was time. She led the small group toward the stage door and knocked.

"Glad you're here," Billie said, opening the door for them.

The stage manager hurried to them. "Kai wants you in the final scene." She spoke into the earpiece she wore. "They're here. I'm sending them to makeup."

Marina had been here before. "We know the way."

They filed through the small backstage area and into the dressing area where a makeup artist was working. As each sat in her chair, she deftly added deeper colors to their cheeks and lips. "That's all we have time for, but you look great."

The prop manager appeared at the doorway with her arms loaded with bouquets. "These are for Marina, Brooke, and Heather. And Mrs. Delavie, you have a corsage." She pinned an orchid to the lapel of Ginger's pink jacket and stepped back. "You all look so lovely and coordinated tonight."

"Kai asked that we wear pink and white," Ginger said. "How lovely this will be from the audience."

Now Marina understood why Kai had asked them to wear

those colors, but she could have explained that she needed them as extras. She thought everyone would have understood, but maybe someone had pushed back before.

Besides herself, Marina realized, feeling a little embarrassed. Well, she was here now.

She smoothed her dress. Fortunately, her chef jacket had protected her sundress. She'd dropped a little aioli near the hem, but it would hardly be visible onstage in a crowd scene. She had also worn a strand of pink-hued pearls Ginger had given her years ago.

Everyone picked up a bouquet of pink roses and white lilies. Marina brought hers to her nose. "These smell wonderful. I guess we're bridesmaids."

The props manager nodded. "And Ms. Delavie will act as the mother of the bride."

"Why, I'm growing younger," Ginger quipped. "Isn't this fun?" She was in her element, too.

"It is sort of exciting," Heather added. "Usually, I'm too shy to stand up in front of crowds."

"You'll be just fine," Ginger assured her. "Everyone will be watching Kai and Axe."

"Sure hope so," Brooke said, twirling her bouquet.

Just then, Kai came in. She looked stunning in a candle-light-colored wedding dress that fit her perfectly. "Wow, you all look fabulous. Who's ready for the best final scene ever?"

Marina was shocked. It wasn't just a dress; it was *the* dress. "You're wearing Ginger's wedding gown as a costume?" By the tightness around their grandmother's mouth, Marina could tell she was not amused that her treasured wedding dress was being used as a costume.

Kai's face colored. "Only for tonight. Since it's opening night and all."

Ginger's eyebrows were shooting toward her hairline. "I hope you'll take good care of it."

"I won't let anything happen to it," Kai promised, fidgeting with a fingernail. "You'll see."

That hadn't been a good decision on Kai's part. Marina could just imagine what Ginger would have to say about it later. Maybe it was only a dress, but the choice was disrespectful to Ginger and their mother's memory. Things like that mattered in their family.

Nevertheless, Kai quickly recovered and went on. "Now, in this next scene, you'll play bridesmaids and family, so you'll be seated on the other side of Billie and Madison. They're serving as Axe's family. We'll have a quick set change, and then we'll guide you onstage to your marks. Ready to go?"

"Lead the way." Lifting her chin, Marina adjusted her attitude. This was a big night for Kai, and the dress was only a dress, after all. Maybe she'd worn it for luck or reassurance. Marina could understand that, and this wasn't the time to argue about it. She gave Kai a quick hug to reassure her. "The audience loves the show."

At that, Ginger nodded her approval. "The gown does look lovely on you, Kai. Now, let's all break a leg."

The stage manager was rotating her hand for them to make haste. With Kai in the lead, they hurried toward the wings. Over her shoulder, she tossed back directorial guidance. "Just act natural, and feel free to react at the appropriate times."

"How will we know?" Heather asked.

Kai laughed. "You'll figure it out."

The lights dimmed, and stagehands guided them onstage. Marina stood where indicated, with Brooke and Heather next to her. They were in character as bridesmaids, and Ginger was seated in front of them. It was a lovely wedding set, and real pink roses surrounded them. The scent was heavenly, but she was surprised they weren't faux flowers.

Trying to relax, Marina sneaked a glance at the audience, though it was difficult to see much except the twinkling canopy of stars above. This was such a special venue that Kai and Axe had brought to life in Summer Beach.

As the lights went up, Ginger winked at her.

This is fun, Marina admitted to herself. They could always count on Kai to bring the sparkles and glitter. She held her bouquet and turned her attention to her sister.

Kai was onstage and in character, worrying that her beloved might miss the wedding. After delivering a few lines, Axe strode on stage and swept Kai into his arms.

Marina was so involved in the storyline that she almost forgot she had a part to play, however small it was.

Axe's voice boomed out in the evening air. "But where's the preacher? He should have been here by now."

At that, Brother Rip emerged from the wings. A gentle giant of a man, he was known by his old surfer nickname, Riptide. These days, he served a flock at the beach, the young surfers who followed the waves, sometimes far from home.

Brooke whispered, "Perfect casting as the pastor."

"That was clever," Marina replied through her stage smile.

With shoulder-length braids and flip-flops, Brother Rip spread his hands. His deep voice with its lilting Jamaican accent rang out. "Dearly beloved, we are gathered here tonight..."

Pausing, he turned from them and toward the audience, breaking the imaginary fourth wall of the theater. He pressed his hands together and added, "To witness the marriage of Kai Moore and Axe Woodson."

A collective gasp swept across those on stage and in the audience. Off to one side, Marina saw a photographer begin shooting photos.

Heather's mouth opened in surprise. "What is Aunt Kai doing?"

"I think this just turned into a real wedding." Marina didn't know whether to laugh or cry out. But this was their

Kai, their beloved wild child, so she thrust her bouquet into the air. "Bravo!"

Kai winked at her and nodded. Her theater friends followed Marina's lead, whooping and clapping. Heather, Ethan, and Brooke did the same. They all improvised in the moment.

In the audience, waves of laughter and calls rippled across the guests.

Brother Rip bowed to the crowd and then turned back to Kai and Axe, who were beaming in the spotlight. The music soared, and the pair began to sing a stunningly beautiful duet, which reminded Marina of "All I Ask of You" from *Phantom of the Opera*.

The audience was mesmerized, and Marina was equally awed by the talent these two possessed. After a few lines, she realized what the song was about. It wasn't just a love song; Kai and Axe were singing their sacred vows to one another.

A lump formed in Marina's throat, and she choked on her emotion—no acting required.

Kai and Axe wore such expressions of pure love that Marina knew they were no longer acting either. As they gazed at each other, it seemed as if their most intimate feelings poured forth from their souls.

Tears of joy sprang to Marina's eyes, and she glanced at Ginger, who was dabbing her cheeks with a handkerchief she'd withdrawn from the pocket of her jacket. Reaching out, Marina clasped her hand.

"This is their finest moment," Ginger whispered.

From what Marina could see of the audience, they appeared awestruck, hanging onto every word, every note, every motion onstage. At the end of the song, Axe slid a narrow band of diamonds onto Kai's finger, and she produced a gold band for him.

Brother Rip raised his hands. "And now, with the power vested in me by the beautiful State of California, the waves that carry us to homeward shores, and the heavens above, I now pronounce you well and properly married."

Kai and Axe embraced with a kiss while cheers erupted onstage and across the crowd. Everyone leapt to their feet, sharing the joy of the moment.

Marina stood with the rest of their family and friends. All were equally surprised and laughing over the turn of events.

At center stage, Kai waved and blew kisses to the crowd. Before turning her back, she called out, "Who's next?" And then, with a swift motion, she tossed her bouquet over her shoulder. According to tradition, whoever caught it would be the next person to marry.

The rose-and-lily bouquet took flight in a high arc. Marina was eager to see who would catch it.

A child's voice rang out. "Get it, Dad!"

The bouquet flew right toward Jack and smacked him in the chest. In a split second, he grabbed it like a football, as surprised as anyone. Laughing, he held the bouquet high above his head like a trophy.

Everyone in the audience laughed, and Jack plucked a white rose and flung it toward Marina onstage, blowing her kisses after it. Jack hefted Leo onto his shoulder, and Leo waved madly at Marina.

"See, we're getting married next," Leo called out to her.

Who could resist such a child?

In the joy and magic of the moment, surrounded by her surprising, loving family and friends, Marina gazed at Jack and Leo with renewed love. Though her resolve was weakening, she struggled to keep it intact. Yet, at that moment, she knew there would always be love between them.

The show continued with the entire cast in the final chorus. At the end, the audience exploded with applause. Along with the rest of the cast, Marina and her family took their bows.

Finally, Kai and Axe trotted back onstage holding hands and took their bows, kissing again for the enthusiastic crowd.

Ginger smiled as she watched them. "All the world loves lovers."

When Kai and Axe returned offstage, their friends congratulated them, and Ginger opened her arms. "Just brilliant! All the fun of a wedding without the stress." She wrapped her arms around both of them.

"There was still plenty of stress," Kai confided. "Imagine planning opening night *and* our wedding. What were we thinking?"

Axe laughed and hugged his bride. "I give all the credit to Kai, my amazing wife."

"Couldn't have done it without you." Kai kissed her husband again. "And wasn't that a magnificent song he wrote?"

"We wrote," Axe added, beaming at her.

They continued talking while the stage lights dimmed, and the audience began to disperse. Marina would have to drive the food truck home, but not just yet.

Heather turned to her, awestruck. "I can hardly believe Aunt Kai and Axe are actually married. And Jack caught the bouquet. Does that mean you're next, Mom?"

Marina laughed. "Jack caught it, not me. You should ask him."

That would be a complicated issue for her children, and after taking into account how Jack lived his life, perhaps it was just as well. One simply didn't change a man. Still, her heart leapt when she spied Jack in the wings.

"And here he is now." Marina went to meet them.

Beside him, Leo was carrying the bouquet, which was so large it trailed on the ground. Jack grinned, his eyes bright with happiness. "I guess it's my choice now."

Marina laughed, but before she could reply, he touched her lips with a kiss that tingled her soul. The softness of his touch and the sweet scent of flowers surrounding her melted another layer of hesitancy.

"You've already said *yes*," Jack murmured, enveloping her in his arms. "In your way, that is."

Marina pulled away and smiled up at him. "But who could possibly top this wedding of the summer?"

16

*E*ven though Jack was already dressed for dinner, he carried the towering stack of pizza boxes to the trash can, which he'd also forgotten to put out for collection last week, and stuffed them in. That was the least he could do, just in case Marina came over after dinner.

Tonight was an important do-over. After Kai's wedding last week, he'd made another reservation at Beaches.

Jack turned and slipped on some muddy muck and nearly went down. Catching himself on the trashcan, he hoped that wasn't something Scout had left behind. Dragging the sole of his polished Italian loafer along a patch of grass to clean it, he thought about the night ahead.

To say he was nervous would be an understatement. He had a lot to make up for, and his future hinged on his ability to persuade Marina. Even though they were officially engaged, he'd felt definite vibes from her that she was pulling away from him.

He should know. The language, the maneuvers—he knew them well. Only he was usually the one employing those tactics.

"Clean enough," he muttered, checking his shoe. Only the

scent of sweet grass and earth filled the air. He'd avoided disaster, yet he still didn't have much time before he had to be at the restaurant. This time, he couldn't be late. All day he'd been thinking about how Marina would react, hoping she could see the love he had for her.

From the far corner of the yard, Scout looked up from his favorite napping spot.

Scout. Jack remembered something. Did he have food and water in his dishes? He'd have to check.

An hour ago, the surfers had finally left the unit over the garage. Jack dreaded seeing what sort of a mess they'd left, but he couldn't be bothered right now.

Cleaning up after his short-term visitors had left him little time to look after his own place. He'd been embarrassed by the state it was in when Marina came over, although the living room hadn't been that bad. He was thankful she hadn't noticed.

Tonight, he had to get their relationship back on track. He made his way into the living room and reached for the faded, red velvet ring box to get a good look at the band that had been his grandmother's. That was the one thing he couldn't forget.

He'd surprise her about the house, too.

Reaching for the light, he flicked it on to get a better look at the ring, but the bulb popped and fizzled out.

He blew out a breath to calm his nerves. He picked up the box and hurried into the kitchen. Inside the original velvet box was a platinum band with a double row of diamonds. Not too small, not too large.

Taking out the ring, he held it up to the light over the kitchen sink. The ring was just as beautiful as he'd recalled. His sister's husband had given her a lovely wedding ring, and she also wore their mother's from time to time. She'd been happy to send this one to Jack.

He hoped the band would fit Marina, but they could size it.

If she liked it.

Turning it from side to side under the light, he thought, *I should clean it for her.* A quick rinse would only take a second and give it a nice shine.

He turned on the water.

Just then, Scout burst through the doggie door and bounded toward Jack. The dog was flying in fast and low on a short landing strip.

"Whoa, boy," Jack yelled in warning, but it was too late to dodge him. Scout skidded and slammed into him, knocking Jack hard against the deep, farmhouse-style sink.

As if in slow motion, the ring catapulted from his fingers on impact and bounced in the sink. Jack pounced, trying to catch it on the rebound, but it sailed up and then straight down, right into the middle of the open drain—clean as a basketball with nothing but net.

"No! No, no, no!" Jack plunged his fingers into the drain after it, cursing himself for not having it covered with one of those stainless steel drain covers he'd been meaning to buy. But it was useless. Quickly, he thrust off the water and banged his fists on the countertop.

"Why? Why now?" he yelled. His frustration level soared off the chart.

Whining, Scout pawed Jack's freshly dry cleaned trousers.

"What?" Then he remembered. The dog's bowls were empty.

Jack gritted his teeth. "You're going to wait a long time for supper after that trick."

As if apologizing, Scout lowered his head and whimpered, pawing Jack's polished loafers—leaving scratches on them.

"Don't do that. Just wait. You'll get your supper as soon as I get that ring."

Jack flung open the cabinet doors under the sink. A lone can of scrubbing powder for the sink and a canister of anti-bacterial wipes sat in his way. Shoving them aside, he glared at the offending pipes, wondering if the ring was caught in the curved trap or if the running water had carried it off to the dark oblivion.

He tugged on the pipes, trying to loosen them, but they were old and stuck, and he didn't have the right tools for the job. He'd done plenty of plumbing work on the farm when he was younger, so he knew what he was missing. A wrench, for starters. Maybe he could go to a neighbor's house and borrow some tools. If they had any.

Scout whined behind him again.

"Okay, but one thing at a time," he snapped. Backing out of the small space, Jack whacked his head on the cabinet. "Ow," he cried, blinking against a flash of swirling stars. He rubbed a rising lump.

He'd nearly knocked himself out. Feeling dazed, he sat on the floor and waited for the sickening feeling to pass. The kitchen clock ticked loudly in the silence.

Seeing the time, he winced. He was late. Patting his pockets, he fumbled for his phone to call Marina but found nothing. He'd probably left it in the bedroom.

Scout crept toward him. Sensing his injury, he licked Jack's face.

"I know you mean well, but not now." Pushing himself up, Jack wobbled toward the cabinet where he kept the dog food. He grabbed the bag and dumped a mound of crunchy morsels into Scout's bowl, and then filled the other one with water.

"There, happy now?" He ruffled the fur around Scout's neck. "Didn't mean to yell at you."

Jack thought about what he could do. Whatever he did, it had to be fast. He made his way to his bedroom and snatched his phone.

"Watch the place for me, Scout," he yelled as he dashed

out the front door, making sure he left it unlocked.

Every minute counted now. As he hurried to his car, he punched Axe's number. "Please, please answer." Fortunately, the amphitheater was dark tonight, but he didn't like to disturb him after hours. However, Jack didn't know anyone else who would know what to do.

"Hello?"

"Thank goodness you answered. It's Jack, and I hate to ask, but I could sure use a favor. I'll make it worth your while."

Quickly, he explained the problem. "And I planned to give Marina the ring tonight at dinner. Five minutes ago, actually."

"Oh, man, you've really messed up."

"I know. Can you give me a hand?"

"Since you're almost family, I'll be right over."

Jack thanked him as he turned the ignition of his old VW van. "And Axe? There's one more favor I have to ask of you."

EXCEPT FOR THE occasion that Jack had hauled Scout out of Beaches, he'd never been to the restaurant, and he hadn't gotten a good look at it then. Jack rushed inside and greeted the maître d', who often went to Marina's cafe.

"Hi, Russell. Is Marina here yet?"

The maître d' glanced at him with a degree of disgust over his tardiness. Jack thought about the night he'd stood up Marina and instantly felt like a louse again. He was wreaking havoc with Russell's reservation list.

"You're late. But at least you're here. Marina's waiting at a table on the patio, but you..." He wrinkled his nose. "You smell like a dog."

Jack sniffed his hand. "Oh, sorry. I had to feed Scout."

"Again with Scout?" Russell shook his head and gestured toward a hallway. "Men's room, that way."

"Thanks."

"And Jack?"

"Yeah?"

"Good luck tonight."

"I think I'm going to need it. Thanks for fitting us in." Jack snapped his fingers. "Say, if a big guy comes in looking for me, could you let me know?"

"You may certainly count on that," Russell replied, smoothing a hand over his perfectly coiffed hair.

After washing off the dog-pizza-rusty-pipe odors, Jack tucked in his shirt and straightened his collar before making his way to Marina. Russell hadn't been able to accommodate him with the best table on short notice, but he had promised a nice table on the small, bougainvillea-draped patio that looked out to the beach.

Although Jack had visited a lot of high-brow establishments all over the world, this was the most upscale restaurant in Summer Beach. Wide windows offered dramatic views of the ocean, and a pianist played on a black, baby grand piano. Everywhere he looked, people were dressed for their special occasions.

Jack stepped into the intimate garden off the main dining room. The romantic setting was perfect.

So was Marina. He paused, staring at her profile. She wore a stylish black sundress that he'd never seen and a strand of South Sea pearls that glowed with the same luminosity as her skin. Suddenly, without seeing him, she stood and picked up her purse.

She was leaving.

Jack's heart almost thudded to a stop. He rushed to her side. "Marina, please sit down. I'm sorry I'm late."

She whirled to face him. "I'm not sure why we're doing this—other than you feel like you owe me dinner here. Let me make this easy for you." She made a move toward the door.

Jack touched her arm. "Can't we just talk? I owe you a lot of explanations." He pulled out a chair for her. After hesitating, she sat down again, although somewhat reluctantly.

He took a seat next to her where he could watch the doorway.

Candles flickered on every table, and twinkling lights lined the arched, stone garden walls. Beyond them, the setting sun flung coral streamers across the sky. He hoped the ambiance would help his cause.

"This is a beautiful place," he began.

She pursed her lips. "Is that all you're going to say?"

That was lame, he admitted, passing a hand over his hair. "My life is…complicated."

"It always is, Jack. I hope Leo is alright?"

"He's fine. My being late tonight didn't have anything to do with him. Just my poor choices."

Marina studied him thoughtfully. "You've been making a lot of those lately. What's going on with you?"

He had no idea where to start. Just then, his phone rang in his pocket. He pulled it out, fumbling with the ringer. It was Axe.

Marina glared at the intruding device. "You're not going to answer that, are you? Unless it's Leo, what could possibly be more important this very minute?"

Jack silenced it. Axe would find the ring or he wouldn't. Answering his call wouldn't make a difference. "Can we just pick up where we left off at the Seashell? You looked so happy for Kai and Axe."

It took a few moments, but she finally smiled. "That was a wonderful night for them, and for all of us. Leave it to Kai to pull off a remarkable wedding."

Jack wanted to say something about their wedding and how it could be just as special, but he figured he should test the shallow waters first. Marina had become evasive, and aside from his apparent penchant for the ill-timed *faux pas*, he wasn't sure why she'd had a change of heart. It seemed the closer he got, the more she pulled away.

Or was it just his imagination?

At any rate, she was smiling now. He flicked a glance toward the doorway, wondering how long it took for Axe to wrench a pipe free. Maybe he should explain what happened tonight.

Yet before he could say anything, a waiter approached their table and explained the specials.

"Those sound delicious," Jack said. "Would you give us a few minutes?"

"Of course." The waiter poured two glasses of champagne, compliments of the chef, and left to check on another table.

However, neither Jack nor Marina touched the flutes.

Jack kept the conversation pleasant on the topic of Kai and Axe as long as he could until Marina finally changed the subject.

"Jack, we need to talk."

"I know we do." He glanced toward the doorway again.

Marina noticed. "Are you expecting someone else?"

"I don't know." Wouldn't Axe have been here by now if he'd found the ring? "I meant, no. Of course not."

Jack was so embarrassed over his gaffe. Marina wouldn't believe it anyway. *I dropped your ring down the sink* was a lot like *The dog ate my homework.* He took her hand and stroked it.

She gave him an odd look and shook her head. "About the point of our last date here—and I use that term loosely because it was only half a date—my half." She narrowed her eyes. "I'd like to know. Had you planned to propose that night?"

Her words were a punch in the gut. "I was. And I admit that I was a jerk. An utter imbecile. A scatter-brained, ill-mannered, inconsiderate jerk."

She folded her arms. "You repeated that last one."

"Well, it bears repeating, doesn't it?"

Jack shifted to get a better look at the doorway. If only Axe would walk in with the prize, the magic talisman that would transform Jack back into the hero in Marina's eyes, not that he deserved that title.

Touching her shoulder, he went on, desperate to regain her confidence in him. "If not for Leo's proposal, we might not be here now."

Marina allowed a small smile. "About that. Leo is such a little sweetheart, and his proposal really touched me, but I don't want you to feel pressured into anything."

"Pressured?" He placed a hand on his chest. "I can think of a plethora of words I would reach for instead—honored, privileged, grateful, awed, thrilled—but pressured isn't one of them."

"You're a regular thesaurus, aren't you?"

Grasping her hand, he kissed it and brought it to his heart. "I've never asked a woman to marry me. I've never even told a woman I loved her. Because I've never felt deep love for a woman until I met you. And that's why I'm so lame at this."

At a table next to them, an elegant gray-haired woman smiled at Jack's words and took her husband's hand.

At least he was reaching someone.

Lowering her gaze, Marina stared at the flickering candle on the table. She seemed to be grappling with her feelings for him, too.

Jack could feel the love she had for him, but something was holding her back. He glanced toward the door again. Just a moment longer, he thought, willing Axe to burst through the door.

Yet, it shouldn't have taken Axe this long. Not with the proper tools.

He wasn't coming, Jack realized, his spirits flagging. The ring might be lost, but Marina was here with him now. He couldn't lose her.

In desperation, Jack began his plea. "This is the part of my speech where I'm supposed to reach into my pocket and—"

"Don't," Marina cried, throwing up her hands.

Jack frowned. "I couldn't even if I wanted to. But isn't that what you want?"

"Wait, what do you mean, *you can't?* I saw an antique ring box at your house."

So she had seen it. Jack pressed a hand to his forehead. "I have a lot of issues you should know about. I can't cook—except for barbecue. I'm sort of a slob—"

"Sort of?"

"I can work on that. But I'm also a klutz. Fumble fingers." He waggled his fingers. Now he was rambling.

Marina narrowed her eyes. "I'm not following."

With a deep sigh, he pushed a hand through his hair. "I need to confess something. I have, or probably had, a very special ring for you. It means a great deal to me—it was my grandmother's—and I'd hoped it would mean a lot to you, too. But tonight, right before I left, I bobbled it."

"You did what?"

"Bobbled it." He waved his hands in front of him in an awkward pantomime.

"What exactly does that mean?"

He lowered his voice in shame. "I dropped it down the kitchen sink."

The woman at the next table looked at him with sympathy.

"Oh." Marina looked down, studying her hands. "Look, Jack. I've been thinking…we don't have to get married. Not right away. Or anytime, really. I won't hold you to your son's proposal."

Jack's heart dropped. "Tonight isn't about the ring. Well, it was, but I'll find another one, just what you want. Let's say that tonight is about us—and our spending our lives together."

Marina grew quiet. Jack didn't know what else to say. He

was pleading for their future, for the life he knew they were meant to have together. How could he win her back?

And then it struck him. She wasn't a prize to claim. Of all the women he'd known, Marina was different. She didn't need him, and he respected her for that. He loved her independence, her will, her determination. And the way she used to look at him, full of admiration for his accomplishments—for stepping up to care for Leo, for bringing Ginger's stories to the page.

Would she ever look at him like that again?

Slowly, Marina shook her head.

Jack pushed away from the table. "You're right. As much as I love you, I can see that I don't deserve you."

17

*I*n the living room of the Coral Cottage, Marina picked up a beautifully framed picture of her parents and turned to Kai. "That was thoughtful of Ginger to go through her photographs for your new home."

Kai selected another one. "I can make copies for you and Brooke."

"Brooke has a lot of family photos already."

"Well, then, for *your* new home, silly." Kai's face was flushed with the optimism of a new life ahead.

"I still have photos in boxes from my place in San Francisco. Besides, a place of my own isn't in the works right now." *If ever*, Marina thought.

"You could get a cute little place nearby. Surely you can manage it with the new food truck."

Kai's perkiness so early in the morning was wearing on her. Her sister was the image of sunshine. She wore a new cotton shift dress speckled with daisies Axe had bought for her, and she'd been chattering about their plans to transform his house into a home for them.

Yet, Marina couldn't begrudge her. She was truly happy

for Kai. The problem was that Marina couldn't stop thinking about what might have been with Jack.

Now that Kai was moving out, the house was strangely silent, and Marina wondered if she should leave Ginger on her own. Especially with Heather's plans to leave for her internship in the fall. Her daughter had finally received confirmation and confided in her. Heather would be interning for a major company in San Francisco. It was a special work-study program, and she had been lucky to be accepted into it. It virtually assured her of a long-term position upon graduation next year.

Kai glanced around. "I need more bags for these photos. Be right back." She dashed off, humming the song from her wedding.

Marina brushed dust from another photo of her parents. It wasn't a formal picture, but one taken of them at the beach. Her father held her mother in his arms, and they were laughing.

That's how Marina always remembered them. They'd had a good marriage. Soulmates, one might say.

Could she have said that about Jack? She hadn't spoken to him since he'd left her at Beaches last week, and more than once, she'd questioned her decision. Worse, Summer Beach was a small town. Even as she assiduously avoided Jack, he seemed to be everywhere.

He was at the Laundry Basket when she picked up her clothes, including the dress she'd worn to Beaches.

He was at the Seabreeze Inn for her book club meeting.

He was at Java Beach when she stopped for coffee.

This past week, Jack had been everywhere but at her cafe.

She'd caught herself looking up from her work in the kitchen when she heard what she thought were his footsteps or Leo's sweet voice, but when she'd turn, the table still reserved for them was empty. She couldn't bring herself to remove the sign from it.

Heather didn't touch it either.

She thought of how hurt Leo must be. Whenever Jack saw her, he just steered the boy away. Leo seemed confused.

Pressing her fingers to her temple, she wondered how a relationship that had once seemed so right had gone so wrong. In her heart, she'd wanted to trust Jack, but all signs pointed to a lifetime of disappointment with an impetuous, irresponsible man-child.

His lifestyle was a disaster, despite what he said. She'd seen it. This was a man who had made a good living from his words—she would not be swayed by the empty promises he made.

Then why was her heart breaking?

"I'm back," Kai said, swinging a reusable shopping bag in her hand. "This is it for today. The trunk is full, and I have to leave room for the cutest pillows I saw at a shop in the village. They'll be perfect for the new couch we've ordered. I have to go back for them as soon as they open. I think I'll buy some flowers to plant along the front walkway, too. How about daisies?"

"To match your dress."

"Oh, right. How funny!" Kai's eyes glimmered with happiness. "I can't wait for you to see the place. Axe and I have been rearranging the house, and we plan to start painting right away."

"I'm happy for you." Marina hugged her. She really meant that, but seeing her youngest sister set up a home of her own was sobering.

"And did I tell you the latest about our honeymoon plans?" Without waiting for an answer, Kai went on. "I've always wanted to see London at Christmas with all the decorations in Covent Garden and around the city. There are so many theater productions in the West End that we'd love to see."

"Won't you spend Christmas here? And what about a holiday performance?"

"Plans change." Kai cleaned the framed photos as she talked. "We might lease out the theater to a touring company for a holiday show. We've promised to see his family, so we'll have to alternate holidays now. Or maybe they'll visit Summer Beach for a break from the winter weather. That reminds me, I have to spruce up the guest bedroom." She laughed. "I didn't realize I'd have so much fun decorating. And for our next home, Axe says he can build our dream house. Because we'll need more room soon."

"Do you mean a baby's room?"

Kai blushed. "I'll have to choose a good understudy."

"Are you thinking of starting a family already?"

"I'm not getting any younger, and we really want a family of little thespians. Won't that be fun?"

"Maybe you can borrow them before you commit." Marina was having a hard time seeing Kai as a mother. "See how you like being a 24/7 mother."

Kai shot her a look of surprise. "What happened to your sense of humor?"

"I'm fine," she replied sharply. "Just busy with the cafe."

"No, it's more than that." She circled her finger toward Marina. "Something's wrong with you. It's Jack, isn't it?"

Her sister finally noticed, but that didn't mean Marina wanted to talk about it. "Why must you always think that Jack is the problem?"

"Because he usually is. Or it's you, but you'd rather think it's him."

Marina shot her a frown. "That doesn't make any sense."

"Of course it does. Think about it." Kai spread her hands in explanation. "You project your fears onto him. You're afraid of being hurt. So, you blame him. Simple, right?"

"Too simple." Marina drew a hand across her face. Kai was getting on her nerves with her pseudoscience. And she needed that second cup of coffee. Her sister had bounced into the house like Tigger out of *Winnie the Pooh* this morning. And Marina felt like Pooh.

Literally.

Kai looked at her with an expression of pity. "At your age, you deserve to be happy."

"At *my* age?" Marina let out a strangled sound. "And you think Jack can do that?"

"Let's see." Kai put a hand on her hip. "We know not having Jack makes you unhappy, so…yes, you should see him again. Case closed."

Marina stuffed the photos into the bag. "I'm through with this overly simplistic conversation."

"Just saying—don't overthink it, toots."

"But when there are red flags—"

"Oh, come on, Marina. The flags you think you see are pale pink at best. He's messy? Hire a housekeeper. Divide the housework. He's unorganized? Get him a wall calendar or an app for his phone. How hard can that be?"

"Says she who's been married five minutes."

"You weren't married to Saint Stan much longer than that."

Marina opened her mouth in shock, then closed it. The old, familiar pain shot to the surface. How dare Kai go there?

Sensing her mistake, Kai pressed a hand to Marina's shoulder. "I'm so sorry. I shouldn't have said that. I know how much Stan meant to you, and he was a wonderful guy. But sweetie, you weren't married that long, and it's been more than twenty years. He wouldn't want to see you alone forever."

"Kai, that's enough—"

"Why not give Jack a chance?" her sister pleaded, doubling down. "I love you, and I don't want to see you miss out on a guy who actually loves you for who you are. The older you get, the rarer they can be. I should know. And you're way ahead of me."

"Excuse me, but did you really say 'way ahead?'" That did it.

Marina shoved Kai's hand aside and spat out her words. "Stop being so smug. Just because you're married now, you think you have all the answers. Just leave. Now."

"I thought you needed some straight talk, that's all. If you hadn't done that for me, I might be married to Dmitri. Or filing for divorce." With a sigh, Kai picked up her bag and left.

Marina turned away, and when she did, she saw Ginger standing in the hallway. She'd been going through other photos in the library, so she must have heard everything. Marina held up a hand. "I'm in no mood for lectures."

Ginger looked weary. "Neither am I. But it's helpful to hear things out loud."

Instantly, Marina's stomach clenched. Some of what Kai said made sense. She drew in her lip. Was she holding Jack to impossibly high standards?

Maybe.

But could she settle for less than perfection?

Blinking, Ginger leaned against the wall and raised a wavering hand to her forehead. "I'm feeling a little warm. Would you get me a glass of water?"

Ginger's voice didn't have the force it usually did. Alarmed, Marina rushed toward her and guided her to the nearest chair. "Are you feeling alright?"

Her grandmother shook her head. "Not…at all."

Marina raced to the kitchen, turned on the faucet, and shoved a glass under the running water. As it filled, she flung open the door. Kai was pulling from the driveway. "Kai!" she screamed. "It's Ginger. Turn around!"

But Kai didn't stop. The windows were up, and she was probably blasting show tunes. Marina grabbed the glass. With water sloshing over the sides, she tore back to Ginger and knelt beside her. "Can you drink?"

Ginger eased it to her lips and took the tiniest of sips. "I might need help to the couch. Perhaps if I lie down, this will pass."

Marina helped her up, but as soon as Ginger took a step, she stumbled and collapsed. Panicking, Marina cradled her in her arms. Ginger needed help; her face was losing its healthy color.

Where was her phone?

Just then, Jack barged into the house and knelt beside her. He wore running shorts, and his face was beaded with perspiration. "What happened?"

"She collapsed." Marina's heart pounded. "I don't know if she's having a stroke or a heart attack."

"Call for help. *Now.*" Without a moment's hesitation, Jack lifted Ginger in his arms and carried her to the sofa, placing her on her side and checking her.

With trembling fingers, Marina tapped the emergency number and gave their address. Panicked tears rushed to her eyes.

The next few minutes were a blur. While Marina was on the phone, Jack tended to Ginger, taking her pulse and checking her airways and breathing. She recalled that he'd had CPR training. In what seemed like both forever and a split second, emergency personnel raced in and took over.

Marina clasped Ginger's hand, which now seemed so cold and small in hers. With a prayer on her lips, she tried to stay out of the way without letting go of her grandmother.

"I'm sorry, ma'am, but we need room to take care of your grandmother," one of the medical responders said to her. They asked a number of questions that Marina tried to answer.

And then, "What happened right before she lost consciousness?"

Through dry lips, she replied, "My sister and I were arguing."

No one said anything, and Marina wished with all her being that she could trade places with Ginger. Feeling lost, she turned to Jack. Fear shrouded her like a blanket of darkness. She pressed her head to his shoulder, and he swept his arms around her.

"She's a strong woman," he whispered.

With her throat closing, Marina could only nod. This was her fault. She ached to take back everything she'd said to Kai that had upset Ginger. Seeing her and her sisters fight had always troubled her grandmother. If only she and Kai hadn't argued. But it wasn't Kai who had started it.

I did this.

Marina's knees buckled at her sick realization, and the room began spinning wildly out of control.

Still, Jack held her.

Within minutes, Ginger lay on a stretcher being loaded into the emergency vehicle. As her eyes fluttered, Marina clasped her grandmother's hands again. "I love you. I love you so much, and I'm so, so sorry for starting that argument with Kai. Please forgive me and be strong for us. I'll stay with you, I promise."

Through an overwhelming fog of emotion that crowded her mind, Marina could hardly process what happened next. Somehow, Jack got her to the hospital. Somehow, Kai and Axe raced to her side. And someone told her that Brooke, Heather and Ethan were on their way.

In an icy waiting room infused with a sharp antiseptic odor, Marina waited, numb to almost everything around her but Jack's protective arms, tenderly holding her together.

She couldn't face losing her grandmother without him.

18

*L*ater that afternoon, Marina smoothed Ginger's hair from her forehead. Thankfully, her grandmother was fully awake now in her hospital bed, and a glow had returned to her face. "I'm so relieved," Marina said softly. "You look like you're feeling better."

Ginger smiled up at her. "I am. But I don't understand why they want to keep me for observation."

"Be happy for that," Kai said, forcing a smile. She sat on the other side of the hospital bed, as she had for the past hour. "They only keep the people they like." She reached across and clasped Marina's hand.

Ginger rested her hand on theirs. "Sisters again?"

"Forever," Marina said, her eyes welling. "Forgive me?"

Ginger's eyes seemed lit with renewed force. "Of course."

When Ginger smiled at them, it was as if the cracks in Marina's heart were mending themselves. She bowed her head and wiped tears of relief from her eyes. As she did, she noticed Kai was doing the same.

The entire Delavie-Moore family had crowded into the small room to keep Ginger company and wait for test results.

The doctor had assured Marina that Ginger seemed healthy; the tests were simply to rule out other conditions.

So far, Ginger's tests had been normal. Marina looked up at Brooke and her family, who'd also been sitting with Ginger. Heather and Ethan were standing with Jack at the door.

Ginger's eyes brightened when she saw them. "Tell the twins to come see me."

Jack whispered to Heather and Ethan, and they approached the bed. "Here, have my seat," Marina said to her daughter.

Ethan perched on the side of the bed, and the two of them began to talk to Ginger.

While they did, Marina moved out of the way. There weren't many places to stand except near Jack. She took the spot next to him, grateful to him for staying with her. She slipped her hand into his.

In the space of a few tense hours, their relationship seemed to have reset itself.

"It's such a relief to see her looking better," Jack said, squeezing her hand. He was still wearing his running gear.

"If you hadn't been out for a run on the beach, I don't know what I would have done."

"I have no doubt that you would have managed. But I'm glad I could help."

Marina smiled up at him with fresh admiration. Jack had been there for her and, most important, for Ginger. He'd dropped everything to take care of them and had called her entire family. When they met at the hospital, he brought food for everyone and kept the younger kids entertained. Even with all that, he made sure Leo could stay with his friend Samantha and her parents so that he could stay at the hospital.

Presently, the doctor arrived, and she wore a smile. "Looks like it's time for you to check out of this posh hotel, Ms. Delavie."

Ginger beamed. "I can't say that I've fully enjoyed my stay, but you and your team have been the consummate hosts. Thank you for all you've done."

As the doctor was leaving, Marina followed her into the hallway to speak to her. "Is there anything else we should know?"

"Your grandmother appears to take good care of herself. All the same, keep an eye on her and make sure she is proactive in her healthcare, nutrition, and exercise regimen."

"I can assure you that she is," Marina said. "She also takes an assortment of herbs and potions that she discovered in her travels around the world to keep her immune system strong."

The doctor nodded. "She told me about that, and I've made a note of it in her chart. I wish more patients had her stamina and wit."

Marina had to ask. "Do you think it was stress that caused this episode?" They had ruled out almost everything. Thankfully, it had not been a stroke or heart attack, but she had lost consciousness.

The doctor explained a little. "Stress certainly has a negative effect on our systems. Try not to upset her unduly. She seems like such a kind woman."

The doctor excused herself, and Marina was relieved that it hadn't been anything more serious.

Kai stepped into the hallway to join them. "I'm really sorry about the things I said." She waved a hand toward Ginger's room. "This was my fault for upsetting her."

"It wasn't just you. Or me." As Marina embraced Kai, clarity rushed over her. "It was everything at once—a perfect storm. This morning, Ginger told me that she hadn't slept well, and she didn't eat anything for breakfast. Going through the photos of Mom had to have an effect on her, even though she accepted her daughter's death with more grace than I will ever comprehend."

"She took such good care of us," Kai said. "I remember that."

"So do I." Marina swallowed. "But the trauma of that accident remains. And then, when we started arguing this morning, that stress that had built up must have taken over. Her body simply shut down."

Kai clasped Marina's hands. "Thank you for sharing that perspective. Still, we're sisters. We should do better. And I promise that I will." She cast a look at Jack. "I appreciate everything you did for our grandmother."

"Of course." He nodded modestly.

After Kai left them, Marina turned to Jack. "You must be concerned about Leo."

"He's fine with Denise and John, but I'll let him know Ginger is okay. He's awfully fond of her."

"Who isn't? My goal is to be like her someday."

"You have her superior genes, that's for sure." Jack tucked a strand of hair behind her ear and kissed her cheek. "I would invite you back to Beaches, but I think that place is bad luck for us. If Ginger is feeling better, would you like to come to my house later this week? I've been cleaning and making changes. I'd really like for you to see the place. And I promise an edible meal."

"I'd like that," she said softly.

By the next day, after Ginger had slept late and eaten well, she was moving about with her usual energy. And by the time the end of the week came and most weekend tourists had left on Sunday, Marina closed the cafe early. She was looking forward to spending the evening with Jack.

Even after seeing him at the hospital, he hadn't stopped by the cafe with Leo. But he'd called to see how Ginger was doing every day.

In preparation for tonight's dinner with Jack at his house, she showered and took extra care with her new hairstyle, though she didn't want to look like she was trying too hard.

She put on a pair of white jeans and a fluttery turquoise top with earrings to match. Yet, she couldn't resist the strappy heels she'd bought to wear for their date at Beaches.

Stepping back from the mirror in her room, she decided her look was nice enough. Not sloppy, not too fancy—just right.

Oddly enough, she wasn't that nervous. Still, when she turned on her heel, she nearly fell. She caught herself on the dresser.

Well, maybe just a little bit nervous. She sucked in a breath and smiled back at her reflection before going downstairs.

Heather and Ginger were playing dominoes in the den. "Wow. You look hot, Mom."

"You must be going out," Ginger said.

"Too much?"

"No, I love those shoes," Heather replied. "Can I borrow them sometimes?"

If her daughter wanted to wear them, maybe they were too young and high for her. "Right. Too much." She turned to go back upstairs.

"Wait." Ginger tapped a finger on the table. "You're only young once. Go have fun." She winked as she picked up another domino. "Fabulous hair, by the way."

Marina couldn't possibly walk the distance in these shoes, so she slid into her Mini-Cooper. Along the way, she stopped at Blossoms. At the flower stand, she bought a tropical bouquet with red ginger flowers, birds of paradise, and glossy ferns. When she pulled in front of Jack's house, she did a double take.

It looked...different.

The grass was cut, the ivy trimmed, and flowers bloomed in glazed pots on the porch.

Was she in the right place? Marina glanced around. Jack's classic VW van was nowhere to be seen. Perhaps he'd cleaned the garage. But she was sure this was the house he'd rented. She stepped from the car.

Carefully, she made her way up the front steps. Before she reached the door, it swung open.

"Welcome to Chez Jacques." Jack wore beige cotton chinos and a white shirt with the sleeves rolled up over his taut forearms, and his feet were bare. "Wow," he said, taking her in with a long, admiring look.

At the sight of him, Marina's heart skipped. She stepped over the threshold. "The yard looks so neat that I wasn't sure I was in the right place. Did your landlord receive complaints from the neighbors?"

Jack gave a self-conscious shrug. "I made a few changes."

The windows were open to the soft ocean breeze. A pale, fluffy new rug sat before the fireplace, where groups of candles on the hearth flickered in hurricane lamps, sweetening the sea breeze. *Jasmine,* she detected, recalling her essential oils. *A known aphrodisiac.*

"I thought you might like these," she said, handing him the flowers she carried.

His eyes twinkled, and he bent his head to admire them. "You brought me flowers?"

"Don't get too excited. Ginger taught me to never arrive empty-handed for dinner." She glanced around. "Is Leo here?"

"He's spending the night with Denise and John. They're taking the kids bowling. I'll put these flowers in water."

She followed him into the kitchen and watched while he brought out an old glass vase that had probably been the previous owner's, but he rinsed it carefully and arranged the flowers. The kitchen was as clean as she'd ever seen it.

"Care for wine? I have a nice bottle."

"I'd like that," she replied.

As he poured two glasses, she took in her surroundings. The floor had been scrubbed, bright new cushions sat on the wooden kitchen chairs, and even the windows looked clean. What had gotten into him?

"You've done a lot of work here." She accepted a glass from him.

"It was time to clean up my act."

"You must have had a good housekeeping team in here."

"Leo and I make a fine team."

"The two of you did this?"

"In this case, I have to take most of the credit. Child labor laws being what they are and all." He lifted his glass to hers and tapped it. "To you," he said, softly meeting her lips.

The kiss was gentle, sending a warm feeling through her. If she had any reservations about tonight, they vanished.

When he pulled away, his eyes lingered on hers. "First course, gazpacho."

"You made it?"

"I watched a couple of videos. It's surprisingly easy with a blender. Throw in the veggies and bam. It's pretty healthy, too."

"And you have a blender now?"

He motioned to a new model on the countertop. "I've learned a lot these past couple of weeks."

"So have I." Ginger's health scare and Kai's words had shifted her thoughts.

They decided to have dinner at the coffee table in the living room, where they could sit on new cushions in front of the candles with a view of the ocean. Jack put on the jazzy music that Marina liked, and she helped him carry dishes and cutlery into the living room, along with the chilled soup and crusty bread with Spanish olive oil.

"And what's this one?" she asked.

"A new salad. It has sliced avocado, feta cheese, balsamic drizzle, and something called little gem lettuce, which I sliced and grilled. Cute little guys, aren't they?"

"You went to the farmers market." And she recognized this recipe. It was one of Ginger's. Was she being set up?

Jack's expression fell. "Is that cheating?"

"Of course not," she replied, touching his chest. "That's where you find the best local produce." Seeing the hopefulness on Jack's face, she decided that if Ginger had helped guide him, she'd have to thank her later.

Marina turned toward the stovetop. "Something smells fabulous. What's this?" She peeked into a covered cast iron skillet.

"Grilled langoustine. I'm keeping it warm in there." He picked up a potholder. "Easy to make, too. If you can grill over a campfire, you can pretty much grill anywhere else. Who knew?"

This was a version of Jack she hadn't seen before. She shook her head with wonder as she followed him back into the living room. "Did aliens abduct you and replace you with a creature from a different species?"

Jack eased dishes onto the table. "I started listening to what you, and other people, had to say."

"Would that other person have been Ginger?"

"She's a wise woman. I've been checking on her while you were working at the cafe."

"I appreciate that," she said, easing onto a silk cushion.

Jack eyed her high heels. "Would you be more comfortable without those? They're beautiful, but I can help you take them off."

She liked the sound of that. "Would you?" She extended a leg.

Touching her ankle with warm hands, he smiled up at her.

Marina watched while Jack undid the tiny buckle on first one shoe, and then the other. Her heart raced as he took his time and placed the high heels carefully to one side.

She folded her legs under her and sipped her wine. "I think I like Chez Jacques much better than Beaches."

"About that. You were right about a lot of things that night."

She cringed. "I don't care about being right anymore."

"Just hear me out," Jack said, smoothing his hand over hers. "In retrospect, I needed that wake-up call. When guys say they can't cook or they don't know how to do laundry, what they're really saying is they don't want to. I can't think of many people who like doing chores, but it sure is nice when they're done. Back on the farm, if you didn't plant the seeds, you wouldn't reap the harvest. I realized I need to be an example to Leo. And to you."

Marina hardly knew what to say. "Not that long ago, you told me you didn't know how to cook unless it was over a campfire."

"That's a macho guy thing to say." He shrugged. "I watched a few cooking videos and talked to your grandmother. She shared some easy tips. You're on your feet at the cafe all day. Just because you're a great cook doesn't mean you should have to carry the entire load. I can certainly learn to shoulder my share. And I need to take better care of Leo."

Marina was pleasantly surprised. "I'll take you up on that."

Between sips of the summer soup, Jack went on. "I have plans for the kitchen, too. For starters, I got a good drain cover."

Marina nearly choked on her wine. It was a shame about the ring, though.

"I sure learned my lesson," Jack said, chuckling. "I'm also installing a dishwasher. And getting a new refrigerator and one of those center islands for more workspace. Axe promised to look at the electrical and plumbing for me."

Marina arched an eyebrow at the list. "Sounds like a lot of money to put into a rental."

"I couldn't agree more." Taking her hand, Jack smiled.

"But it's no longer a rental. You're looking at the new owner. And that means no more surfers in the studio out back."

"You bought it?"

"When I was turned down for a loan, Bennett talked to the owner. Garrett is a great guy—he grew up in this house—and he agreed to carry the loan for me. It's not much more than rent."

"Can you manage it?"

"Let's just say it's been a busy week." Jack grinned.

Curiosity rose in her. "What else happened?"

Jack tore a piece of bread and dipped it in olive oil. As they ate, enjoying the langoustine and the salad, he told her the story of the guy he'd overheard at the cafe.

Marina was shocked. "Were you frightened?"

"At first, until I ran into him at Fisherman's Wharf. I recognized his voice. Turns out, he's an intern for a top producer. But not a very honest one."

Jack continued the story. "I figured if this was such a hot story right now, it might be time to pitch it again. I got in touch with my agent, and tonight we're celebrating. I signed an option this morning for a new series, and the attorneys are working on the full contract right now. The producers are interested in what they're calling the next phase, which is the research I had that never made it into the trial. Because of that, essentially, I'll get to write my own ticket."

"Oh, Jack, I'm thrilled for you."

"And the best part is, I get to stay right here in Summer Beach." He cleared his throat and reached into his pocket. "With you, if you'll have me."

He withdrew the faded, red velvet ring box that she recognized.

Marina gazed at him in astonishment as he opened the velvet carrier, and a diamond band twinkled in the candlelight.

"Oh, it's so lovely," she breathed. But more than that, Jack loved her, and he was committed to staying in Summer Beach.

"This was my grandmother's."

She was surprised. "But I thought it was lost."

"Almost. It was a messy job, but Axe rescued it. This ring has been through a lot more than that, though. The woman who wore it first was a creative, determined, beautiful woman. You remind me of her in the best possible ways. You can choose whatever ring you want, but if you like this one, and what it means between us..." Jack lifted it from the box. "You don't need me, Marina Moore, but you would do me the greatest honor and make me the happiest—"

Marina cut off his words with a kiss. In her heart, this is why she was here. To step into their future together. As a torrent of happiness gushed through her, she cradled his face in her hands. "Yes," she whispered.

Jack enveloped her in his arms, and for the first time in years, Marina felt like she'd found a place that her heart could call home. Tears of joy filled her eyes.

Smiling, Jack peppered her face with kisses. "Then the only questions that remain are when and where?"

*a*t nearly four on a Saturday afternoon, leisurely lunch patrons were finally filtering from the cafe. In the kitchen, Marina glanced at an order, double checking as she plated a spinach salad with strawberries and feta cheese. *Balsamic dressing on the side, no onions.*

Across from her, Heather slid a note across the kitchen counter.

"What's that?"

"A note from your biggest fan." Heather nodded toward the salad. "Is that for table four?"

Marina traded the salad for the note. "Take it away. Any more orders?"

"Nope. It's finally slowed down. It's incredible how much business we get from the food truck."

"That's the power of mobile advertising."

Cruise appeared from the back, wearing a bright coral-colored T-shirt.

Heather looked up at him and smiled. "Nice T-shirt."

"These just came in." Cruise grinned amicably and turned toward the deep fryer.

Marina noted the exchange. Her daughter and Cruise had

become friends. "The new shirts are in the back. Grab a few for yourself." Marina was pleased at how the new Coral Cafe logo looked on the shirts. She leaned against the counter and unfolded the note.

How about an underwater scuba wedding?

Shaking her head at such absurdity, Marina stepped onto the outdoor patio. She spied Jack at his usual table, and Kai sat with him. The two looked like they were cooking up trouble, and she wondered which one of them had come up with this latest idea.

Jack often brought his laptop to write at the cafe. His latest project was going well, and she was happy for him. At last, they were both doing what they loved.

She made her way across the patio, pushing in chairs and picking up errant bits of napkins and wayward fries as she went, tossing them into the trash.

A scuba diving wedding, indeed. Still, Marina had to laugh about it, even though they hadn't made much progress on their wedding plans these last few weeks.

She hadn't realized how rapidly her business might grow this summer. Jack had been patient, but she wanted to move the wedding plans along. Juggling both was a challenge, but she was managing. Barely, some days.

The food truck had done more than create a new income stream; it was a mobile advertising machine that drew people to the Coral Cafe and exploded her business. Customers were now waiting in line for tables. This was a different crowd; they weren't only seasonal tourists but also people from surrounding communities who'd seen the food truck at a venue.

Marina sent out a daily crew in Coralina. The truck and its crew visited beaches, art festivals, outdoor concerts, and weddings. Cruise had proven to be an excellent cook, and the team liked the variety of serving at different venues. Heather and Cruise worked especially well together. Marina continued to alternate with him on the truck so she could gain firsthand knowledge to refine their mobile menu.

As Judith had mentioned, food trucks for weddings were gaining in popularity. While most of the wedding parties contacted her for the fresh California casual fare the cafe was becoming known for, she had also served a variety of themed wedding events. They'd handled everything from a Renaissance wedding with roast beef and ale to a vegan event with grilled vegetables and sustainably sourced ingredients. With a front-row seat to so many different options, Marina was taking notes for her wedding.

So was Jack, but in an effort to find an interesting venue that would be easy to manage, they hadn't been able to agree on anything.

Marina took a chair next to Jack, who was scribbling in a small spiral notebook. She glanced between him and her sister. "Underwater, really? Which one of you came up with that gem?"

Jack and Kai burst out laughing. "Hear me out," Jack said. "It would be like Jacques Cousteau, only I'd be *Jack* Cousteau, capturing the lovely mermaid, Marina."

She slapped his hand playfully. "Be serious. Jacques Cousteau was a renowned oceanographer. Do you even scuba dive?"

"I've learned my way around the kitchen. I'm sure I could manage the ocean floor."

Kai's eyes widened. "Do you know how many divers get married undersea?" She waved a hand in the air as if painting a picture. "Wedded amid the fish and coral—just think of how great that would be for your branding. I bet lifestyle editors and social media would love that headline: Coral Cafe owner is married among the coral. It would be a great feel-good piece."

Marina glared at Kai. "Our wedding is not a public relations opportunity. Besides, think about Ginger." Their grandmother was doing well now, but she didn't want to risk her health.

"Ginger would probably embrace the adventure," Kai said, grinning. "She used to dive."

Jack rubbed his chin in thought. He had been pitching all sorts of ideas for their ceremony, from a destination wedding in Italy—that was vetoed due to cost and distance for guests—to his sister's farm in Texas—another veto due to the August heat and lack of nearby accommodations.

Snapping his fingers, he leaned forward. "How about we get married on the water's surface? Mitch has his charter boat that can handle our sizable crowd. We could cruise the shoreline at sunset."

Marina shook her head. "Some guests suffer from motion sickness. Heather, for one."

"Ditto," Kai said, sheepishly sliding up her hand. "Not always, but that sure could ruin a dress."

"Can't have that." Jack crossed off the entry on a list in his notebook.

Marina peered at the list. Every line was scratched out. "We sure have been through a lot of ideas."

"And if you want to get married before fall, time is running out," Kai said.

Jack squeezed Marina's hand. "I'd rather not wait."

"Agreed." Now that they had decided to marry, each day they were apart seemed like a loss. Marina longed to move in with him and Leo.

Jack fumbled with a small tin and popped one of his curiously strong peppermints into his mouth. He held out the tin. "Want one?"

She shook her head, but she recognized his crutch. "Feeling nervous?"

He quirked the side of his mouth. "As off the wall as it was, I see that Kai and Axe had the right idea for their wedding. Don't think; just do."

Kai broke out in laughter. "Sure, it was a breeze. That is, after I wrote the script. And then we had to swear the photographer and Brother Rip to secrecy, arrange flowers and rehearsals, and so on. We just didn't tell guests and family."

Jack snapped his fingers. "That's it. We could elope. How about a Las Vegas drive-through chapel? Elvis could officiate. Maybe we could find a room with a heart-shaped bathtub."

Thinking about Kai's extravagant onstage wedding, Marina wasn't sure what she wanted other than to have family and friends with them. "Las Vegas is fun, but I'm not feeling the vibe."

"Neither am I." Jack crunched another breath mint. "But at this stage, I'd go for that just to get it over with."

Marina sat back. "You can't mean that. Don't you want something romantic and meaningful?"

"When I already have you, that seems redundant." He flashed a grin. "Justice of the Peace, County Courthouse?"

"No," Kai cried, alarmed. "Not a government office building."

Marina tapped the table in front of Jack. "You're not getting off that easy. I'm wearing a beautiful dress somewhere equally memorable. That's all I ask. We'll keep looking—unless you like one of my ideas."

Jack raised his brow. "A hot air balloon? A pumpkin patch? A ladies' spa?"

"Men go to those, too," Marina replied, folding her arms. "The grounds are beautiful."

"But people wander around in bathrobes." Jack tore off the page, crumpled it, and tossed it onto the table. "This is impossible."

Marina took his hand and stroked it. More than anything, she wanted this to be a celebration of their commitment. "Why not something closer to home?"

· · ·

198 | JAN MORAN

As soon as Jack's sister walked from the San Diego airport terminal, Marina recognized her. Liz greatly favored her brother, with thick, shoulder-length brown hair and an easy gait. Only the accent was a little different. Jack had lived away from Texas for a long time.

Marina was glad they could come with just a week's notice. She extended her hands to Liz. "You'll have to tell me all about your brother while I still have time to back out."

Liz laughed. "He's promised to pay me well to keep my mouth shut. But luckily for you, I'm a woman of independent means. Let's talk."

Like Jack, Liz had a quick wit and a good sense of humor. She was clearly a strong woman capable of herding rowdy children and livestock. Marina liked her instantly.

Jack slung his arms around Liz, her husband, Ryder, and their children. He called out to Leo, "Come meet your new cousins."

Mary Beth, the oldest, was fifteen. Mack was a year older than Leo, and Joey was a year younger.

Leo seemed at a loss for words, which surprised Marina. With all that Leo had faced in his young life, she often thought of him as more mature, but underneath he could still be a bashful child, especially when faced with so many new people.

Jack nudged him. "Remember what we talked about?"

With a shy smile, Leo said, "Anyone want to go to the beach? We can take my dog, Scout."

"May we, Mom and Dad?" Joey asked, jumping up and down.

"You bet," Ryder said. "That's really why we came—to bring these land-locked kids to the shore. Who cares about old Uncle Jack, anyway?"

The two men punched each other in the arms, laughing.

With a warm smile, Liz reached for Marina's hand. "Our grandmother's ring looks beautiful on you."

"Jack told me you'd been keeping it for a special occasion. I can't tell you how much I appreciate you parting with it."

"This is that special occasion. I just didn't know it until Jack called."

"You didn't want to keep the ring for Mary Beth?"

"My daughter can have my mother's wedding ring if she likes, but she'll probably want to choose her own. That's how kids are these days. And I like the thought of you wearing it. Jack is right; you do remind me of our grandma Josephine."

Marina was relieved that Liz hadn't minded parting with a family heirloom. She loved the ring and the family history it represented.

Under sunny skies, they made their way to the parking lot. They'd brought Jack's classic VW van, which had plenty of room for all of them, along with their luggage. They all piled in and buckled up.

"What a charming van," Liz said, admiring the interior's retro renovation. She leaned forward to talk to Marina. "Did you know Jack had planned to drive through Texas in this on his way back to New York?"

"Then, the next we heard, he never made it out of Southern California." Ryder chuckled. "He picked up a dog, a kid—and soon, a wife. That's a lot of anchors on this shore."

"I'm happily anchored," Jack said, bumping Ryder's fist.

"That's my man," Ryder replied.

Marina and Liz laughed at the men's banter.

"We've both had a lot of changes," Marina added, placing her hand on Jack's shoulder as he drove.

"All for the best, it sounds like," Liz added. "We're so happy to welcome you to the family."

By the time they arrived in Summer Beach, Marina felt like she'd known Jack's relatives for a long time. They were easy to get to know, and they all enjoyed teasing Jack.

After they arrived at his home and got out of the car, Jack threw an arm around his sister. "I shouldn't have introduced you to my bride until after the wedding. You might scare her away."

"We've only just started," Liz said. "Where's your sense of humor?"

Marina watched as they laughed and walked together, catching up. She was happy to see that Jack bore his sister's teasing in a good-natured manner. Seeing how they treated each other with respect and love was reassuring to Marina.

As for accommodations, Jack settled the boys in the VW van, which had a sleeping area, while Marina showed Mary Beth to Leo's clean room. Liz and Ryder were pleased to have the upstairs suite over the garage to themselves. While they likened the splatters to a Jackson Pollack painting, Marina and Jack decided to name the art studio after Garrett's father, Garrett Rivers, Sr.

Jack had thoroughly cleaned the studio suite after the last guests, and Marina had bought new sheets, towels, and a tablecloth. She'd created an airy sanctuary with a few decorative pieces and woven rugs.

As they were walking back to the cottage, Jack took her hand. "You've been a huge help. I couldn't have done all this without you."

"You're not as helpless as you think," Marina said. Over the past few weeks, she and Jack had been having deep discussions about each other's expectations. "You organized the house, and I did the shopping. That's the fun part."

"That's what I dread. Don't minimize your contributions."

"Now you sound like Ginger. Have you two been talking?"

Jack smiled and squeezed her hand. "I'm a good listener when I put my mind to it."

LATER THAT EVENING, they all arrived at the Coral Cottage, where Ginger had invited them for dinner. This was an opportunity for Jack to introduce his family to Ginger.

Brooke arrived with her husband Chip and their boys, who joined Leo and his newly discovered Texas cousins, as he called them, on the beach. After some evaluation, Leo realized that Brooke's boys would also be cousins by marriage.

Marina thought it was heartwarming that Leo, who had craved an extended family, now had six new cousins. And probably more on the way from Kai and Axe.

Her sister and her new husband weren't there, as they were busy with a performance at the Seashell. Marina's new staff, headed by Cruise, was managing the food truck at the Seashell tonight. *Belles on the Beach* was popular, and Kai and Axe joked that they remarried in every performance, although another actor had taken Brother Rip's place.

As they gathered around the dining room table, Ginger welcomed Jack's family. "How nice to meet you all. Jack is fortunate to have such a loving family. And I think we'll have many good times ahead."

"Here, here," everyone chimed in.

Marina and Jack enjoyed watching their families get to know each other over a dinner of lasagna and salad that Brooke had brought and the tiramisu that Marina had made the day before. This wasn't a rehearsal dinner because the wedding they'd planned was casual, and Marina and Jack saw no need for a trial run. They would all meet tomorrow at the cottage.

After dinner, as Marina and Jack washed dishes and Brooke and Chip cleared the table, Ethan and Heather barged into the kitchen. Ethan's hands were on his hips, and Heather was frantically gesturing behind him.

"No, please don't tell her now," Heather pleaded.

"What on earth?" Marina turned with alarm.

Ethan began, "I've been wanting to talk to you about this guy, Mom.'"

"About what?" Marina asked, surprised at the tone of his

202 | JAN MORAN

voice. Her chest tightened with concern. The night before their wedding? This could be trouble.

Wagging a finger at Jack, her son went on. "I want you to know that I didn't trust this guy when I first met him."

"Now, wait a minute," Jack said as soap bubbles dripped from his hands. "I thought we'd talked about this."

Marina shot looks at Jack and Ethan. "Obviously not enough. What's going on?"

Just then, Heather and Ethan burst out laughing. "Fooled you," Heather said.

Ethan chuckled. "She put me up to it."

"Oh, you two. You're as bad as he is." Marina jerked a thumb at Jack.

"We just want you to know we're really happy for you," Heather said.

Marina was relieved. Earlier, her children had enthusiastically endorsed her marriage to Jack, saying they adored Jack and didn't want to see her alone.

Jack tossed them a pair of hand towels. "Just for that, you're on work duty."

Though the twins grumbled good-naturedly, they picked up the freshly washed dishes and began drying them.

"Seeing you all together is the best wedding gift I could have asked for," Marina said. She only hoped that tomorrow would dawn with happiness and clear skies.

20

"*N*ow you can look," Brooke said, removing her hands from Marina's eyes.

"Wow, it's gorgeous." Marina gazed around the private patio behind Ginger's cottage in awe. The entire area was shrouded with lacy pink bougainvillea and surrounded by yellow hibiscus shrubs, but her sisters had transformed it with lights, flowers, and vibrant coral tablecloths.

"The fairy lights were my idea," Kai said, spinning under the canopy of palm trees laced with twinkly lights. "Ethan and Ryder brought tables and chairs from the cafe patio."

"They were so helpful," Brooke added, hooking a thumb in her overalls. "I was afraid we wouldn't finish in time. And we need plenty of time to change. Especially our bride."

"What you've done here means so much to me. Sometimes it's hard to let go of all the little details." Marina's heart quickened with anticipation. Today was the day her life would change. She'd hardly dared imagine having a partner again. Yet, happily, here she was.

"This is your day," Brooke said, smiling. "You do so much. Let others do the work while you relax and enjoy it all. You'll remember this day for the rest of your life."

"Honestly, it's more than I imagined."

When Marina had thought of being married on the beach, she'd canceled the idea because she didn't want Ginger to feel like she had to do anything. Marina was still being cautious about her grandmother. Between the cafe, the food truck, and Jack's family in town, Marina knew she wouldn't have time to do much. But Kai and Brooke had stepped in to help.

"This isn't everything." Kai smiled. "Keep looking."

On the stone fireplace that anchored one end of the patio, her sisters had put a photo of their parents in a place of honor. Marina walked toward it. "Now I see Mom and Dad." Still feeling their love within her, she kissed her fingertips and touched the photo. "Thank you for doing this."

Everything in this cottage held memories. Marina ran her hand along the smooth stones surrounding the fireplace.

Ginger and Bertrand had built this together as a young couple. Mosaic tiles in shades of coral and polished to a sheen covered the hearth. Even in the summer, if an unseasonal front of cold air crept in, they could rouse a fire against the evening chill.

Her sisters had taken care of all the details, but in truth, keeping busy helped calm her mind. Not that Marina was nervous—well, maybe a little. *What if a sudden rainstorm sweeps in?* More than anything, she was excited about her life ahead.

She and Jack had already moved most of her clothing and incidentals to his home. After his family left, she would have the rest of her household items from storage delivered.

Kai checked the time. "Ginger wants us to dress in her suite."

Before leaving the patio, Marina took a last look. The ceremony was a scant few hours away. She made her way upstairs with her sisters to Ginger's suite.

Their grandmother was already dressed in a flowing, soft coral caftan with strands of coral at her wrists and neck. She greeted Marina with a hug. "Kai and Brooke will help you dress, and Brandy from Beach Waves is coming by to make sure your hair is picture perfect."

"It seems like a lot of trouble to go to." Marina bit her lip. She wasn't used to being doted on. "Jack sees me at my worst and still loves me as I am." After working long days at the cafe, her hair and clothes often picked up the kitchen aromas. She'd learned that a long bath at the end of a day was more than a restorative treat; it was a necessity.

"Actually, this is Jack's treat, dear. He arranged for Brandy to do your hair. He wants you to feel pampered today." Ginger embraced her again. "Trust me, when you're my age, you'll be glad you have photos of this day, and you'll marvel at how lovely and young you looked. Because you are, my dear. Now, go take your bath. We're expecting Venus to emerge."

Marina smiled. "I'll see if I can find her in the tub."

When she walked into the bathroom, she was delighted at the scene that her grandmother had set for her. Fluffy white towels were stacked by the large tub, along with an assortment of fragrant bath gels and her favorite facial scrubs and masks. In the low light, candles flickered at the vanity and beside the tub. A flute of chilled champagne rested on a silver platter, and a mix of love songs played softly in the background.

Marina couldn't remember when she'd been so spoiled.

After a leisurely bath, she emerged, feeling very much like a goddess. She put on a silk robe that Ginger had left for her and wrapped her hair in a towel. She wondered what Jack was doing now.

As she padded into Ginger's suite, she saw that Heather had joined Kai, Brooke, and Ginger. They were chatting with Brandy about the latest hairstyles. Marina greeted the stylist, whose shiny cognac locks were brushed into a high ponytail that fell dramatically to her shoulders.

"Here's our star now." Kai patted a small chair in front of Ginger's vanity, and Marina sat down.

Brandy swept a cape over Marina's shoulders. "What would you prefer? Updo or falling softly on your shoulders?"

"I'd like it swept from my face and secured against the breeze, but I'd also like to showcase the coloring magic you did."

"Absolutely. We can do that." Brandy removed the towel from Marina's hair and reached for her hairdryer and brush.

Kai and Brooke chatted while Brandy worked. Heather and Ginger disappeared into the closet where Ginger kept her jewelry vault. She'd told Marina that she would let her choose just the right accents for her dress.

"I brought my bag of tricks, too," Kai said, opening her stage makeup kit.

Marina eyed the vivid makeup assortment with skepticism. "Please don't make me look like I should be onstage."

"Trust me," Kai said. "I'm a professional."

"That's what I'm afraid of. I'd like for Jack to recognize me."

Brandishing a makeup brush, Kai just laughed.

When Brandy and Kai had finished their artistry, Marina opened her eyes. Brandy had loosely braided a section of her hair by her face and secured it with one of Ginger's antique hair ornaments. Soft waves cascaded over her shoulders. And Kai's makeup was sublime.

Marina hardly recognized her reflection in the large oval mirror. She looked like herself, of course, only better than she'd thought possible without being overly made up.

More like she'd had a good night's rest, a fabulous vacation, and a clock that spun backward.

"Wow, Mom." Heather whistled. "You're gorgeous. Aunt Kai, can you do something with my makeup, too?"

"Of course, sweetie. Step right up."

Brooke helped her with Ginger's dress, which Kai had cleaned and insisted on having altered to fit Marina. And surprisingly, it did. The long, sheer lace overlay added just the right touch of feminine elegance.

Marina turned to her grandmother. "What do you think?"

Ginger clasped her hands to her chest. "Exquisite. This brings back so many wonderful memories."

"This is only its fourth trip down the aisle—or across the stage." Marina turned to Heather. "Maybe Heather will want to wear it next."

Her daughter's eyes brightened. "That could be a while, Mom."

"You never know what tomorrow might bring." Marina thought about the day she'd met Jack. What she'd thought was one of the worst days of her life turned out to be the best. She wouldn't know it until much later, though.

Marina's heart was beating fast again, and she pressed a hand to her chest. It wouldn't be long now.

Marina had asked Heather, Kai, and Brooke to choose coral-colored sundresses in styles that accented their best features. While they changed, Ginger unrolled a felt jewelry roll at the vanity.

"Pearls and diamonds are always right, my dear. Or you might prefer the coral." She lifted a delicate necklace with a carved pink coral rose. "This belonged to Sandi."

Marina admired the delicate pendant. "I remember Mom wearing that."

"It was mine, and I gave it to her on her sixteenth birthday."

Marina clasped the necklace and touched the rose with reverence, wishing her parents could be there. She added one of Ginger's fine pearl necklaces to frame the coral pendant and discreet, diamond-studded pearl earrings.

"Just right," Ginger said, touching Marina's shoulder. "What a lovely bride. Look at yourself in the mirror."

Marina gazed at her reflection in Ginger's full-length

mirror. Overwhelmed with emotion, she dabbed her eyes. This was a day she'd once thought might never come again.

Ginger held out a hand to her. "It's time, my dear."

Marina took her grandmother's hand. She could hardly wait to see Jack.

WITH THE CORAL Cottage behind her, Marina clutched a bouquet of roses, peonies, and ranunculus, all in shades of coral. Her friend Imani from Blossoms had created the bouquet and other floral decorations.

Taking a step onto the sand, Marina approached the very spot where her mother had married years before and where she and Kai and Brooke had played as children. A tall arch decorated with coral roses was secured on either side of the flat rock that jutted toward the sea.

They'd all left their sandals and shoes by the rear door and changed into the wedge-heeled, rhinestone-encrusted flip-flops Kai had bought for them. Heels would only sink into the sand.

Ethan escorted Ginger first. Their family and friends were already gathered by the rock, and they turned and smiled at her.

"You're the mermaid queen today," Kai said. "No contest at all."

Marina admired the women who walked with her, those she was fortunate to call sisters. For all their petty arguments, she was proud and honored to have them beside her today.

Jack's family and many friends from Summer Beach were there. Ivy and Bennett, Shelly and Mitch, and Leilani and Roy stood to one side. Jen and George stood with Vanessa and Dr. Noah, who had just returned from their honeymoon.

From the top of the rock, Jack beamed at her. He wore an intricately embroidered, white linen *guayabera*, a traditional shirt worn over loose trousers. The wind ruffled his thick hair, and he appeared confident and sure of the step they were taking today.

Standing beside Jack was Brother Rip, facing the sea as if drawing all its energy to bless this marriage. Perched on a stool on one side, Bennett softly strummed a guitar.

Marina thought everything was perfect.

After slipping off her wedged flip-flops, she lifted the hem of her grandmother's wedding gown and stepped onto the long, flat stone on the beach where her parents had pledged themselves to each other so many years ago. Beneath the rich satin fabric, Marina planted her bare feet on the sun-warmed rock, feeling the sand beneath her feet just as her mother had.

The breeze swept back her hair, which fell past her shoulders. The satin dress and the long, sheer lace overlay rippled in the wind.

Their family gathered around them. Next to Ginger stood Chip, his three boys, and Axe, her new grandson-in-law. Ryder held the lead for Scout, who wore a handsome coral bandana around his neck and seemed to understand the importance of the celebration. Liz gathered with their children.

Brother Rip turned to them with a peaceful expression on his face. His deep, lilting voice rumbled against the mesmerizing rhythm of the ocean. "I sense your angels are with us today. They have been waiting for this moment."

At his words, Marina felt the reassuring presence of her parents, as if time separating them had somehow melded, and they were reunited at this spot by the sea. Warmth radiated through the soles of Marina's feet.

She glanced at Ginger, whose eyes were closed. Her grandmother wore a peaceful smile as if she were somehow communicating with her beloved daughter. When she opened her eyes, they were as clear as Marina had ever seen.

"We love you," Ginger whispered, placing a hand over her heart.

"And I love you, and Mom and Dad, forever." Marina

hugged Ginger, holding her tightly and feeling her love.

Beside her, Kai and Brooke had tears in their eyes as if they had felt something, too.

After a moment, Jack cleared his throat and offered his hand. Perhaps he felt the presence of his angels, too.

Marina slid her hand into his. At that moment, she knew in her heart that she and Jack had been destined to be joined here.

Beside Marina stood Heather and Ethan, and next to Jack was Leo, beaming at her. If not for Leo, they might not be standing here today. Marina winked and blew him a kiss.

Clasping Jack's hand firmly in hers, she faced the distant horizon with him, feeling as if their future was opening to them. All they had to do was step into it.

Ginger stood with them, her face wreathed with a smile and joy in her eyes. Her grandmother's approval of this marriage meant everything to Marina because she trusted her judgment. Even though, as Ginger was fond of saying, *you're the ones who will have to live together and make it work.*

As Marina held Jack's hand, the warmth radiating from it was like nothing she had ever known. It wasn't only the heat of his palm; she felt intense energy growing between them.

At that moment, Jack stared at her in amazement and admiration. "Do you feel that, too?"

"It's incredible." As emotion welled in her eyes, Marina passed her bouquet to Kai and joined both hands with Jack.

This was their moment. After pledging themselves to each other, Marina met Jack's lips in a magical kiss that seemed to suspend time.

A moment later, their family and friends broke out with cheers. Marina and Jack paused to take photos with everyone. Later, when Marina would look at the photos taken of the day, she knew she would feel all the joy and happiness of that moment.

Ginger was right. They even made sure to have a photo

taken with Scout.

Jack snapped his fingers. "Come on, boy. It's your turn."

As Marina and Jack were posing with Scout, a seagull swooped low and landed by the rose-covered arch. Scout eyed the bird with a wary look. As if dared, the gull pecked at the flowers, taunting him.

Jack held his dog's collar. "It's okay, boy. Just smile for the photo."

But Scout had other ideas. Suddenly, he broke free and bounded toward the interloper, throwing Jack off balance.

Quickly, the gull lifted off, its great span of wings soaring on the breeze.

"Scout, come back," Marina called.

Yet, Scout couldn't stop. Skidding in the sand, he careened toward the flower-encrusted arch. And then, as if in slow motion, the arched structure fell away from the crowd. No one could have stopped it.

"Timber," Jack yelled, and everyone turned to look.

The structure tumbled toward the sand and crashed, sending a spectacular shower of rose petals whirling in an onshore gust. Petals floated down upon the crowd like sweet confetti.

Leo flung his arms around Scout while Marina and Jack embraced in a whirlwind of fragrant rose petals, laughing and kissing.

"That's perfect," the photographer said happily.

"Everything is perfect with you in my life," Jack replied, gazing into Marina's eyes. "Even when it's not."

"I couldn't agree more." Marina felt like the luckiest woman in the world.

Kai clapped her hands to get everyone's attention. "Let's go toast this happy union."

Leo and the other boys picked up the pieces of the broken arch and made their way to the patio.

The party afterward was everything Marina wanted,

surrounded by family and their Summer Beach friends.

"That was just as lovely as your mother's wedding," Ginger said, gently touching the neckline of the wedding dress she'd worn decades ago. "We're all part of this fabric now."

Marina smoothed a hand over her grandmother's. "I think of our family as a tapestry woven of strong thread."

"What a lovely thought." Ginger's eyes misted. "And every generation embellishes the story." She nodded toward Heather. "Your daughter might be next. You'll take good care of this dress for her?"

Hardly daring to think that far ahead, Marina embraced her grandmother. "We both will."

She and Jack spent the evening laughing with friends and family who toasted them countless times with Ginger's vintage crystal. For once, Marina hadn't cooked, and neither had Ginger or Brooke. Following Ginger's recipes, Mitch had prepared the seafood buffet dinner with fresh ocean catch and the freshest of farmers market vegetables. Ginger's long-time friend from the market, Cookie O'Toole, had made the cake using a delicious mango-lemon recipe.

As the night wore on, a soft mist cooled the beach, and stories flowed around the outdoor fireplace. Marina could hardly imagine a better ending to the day.

Almost.

She reached a hand to Jack. "Ready to return to where we first met?"

He folded her hand in his and kissed it. "You know I am."

After saying their goodbyes and leaving the Coral Cottage, Marina and Jack drove the short distance to the Seabreeze Inn.

Ivy had given them a key and told them to park in the car court whenever they arrived. She had reserved the best room at the grand old beach house for them, one that had been the former owner's suite and had a magnificent ocean view that stretched to the horizon.

Marina and Jack parked the Mini-Cooper in the car court. With their arms encircling each other, they strolled across the expansive patio and past the Neptune-inspired pool glistening with moonlight. Beyond the pool was a path planted with tropical flowers that led to quarters converted into guest rooms.

They both stopped, staring at a spot just outside a door to a room.

"Right there," Jack said, nodding toward a place on the path. "That's where we met."

Marina remembered. "And I thought, now there's a man with eyes too blue to be trusted."

"I'm glad you could see past that and into my heart." Jack kissed her forehead and led her up the ramp to the rear of the house.

As he turned the key in the door, Marina smiled at another memory. On the day they met, she'd limped out on crutches after spraining her ankle. Ginger had been away, and Marina had fled the disaster that had been her life in San Francisco so quickly she'd left her keys to the cottage. Little did she know that action would lead to this beautiful night, with their new life stretching before them.

"I remember asking you to open this door for me," she said, sliding her hand along her new husband's chest.

Jack's eyes sparkled brighter than the stars. "At last, I can do what I wanted that day."

"Which was?" she asked, teasing him.

Brushing his lips on hers, Jack swept her into his arms and carried her over the threshold. A smile lit his face. "Think of the time we could have saved if I'd done that then."

Marina threw her head back and laughed. "But what a wonderful journey it's been."

The End

AUTHOR'S NOTE

Thank you for reading *Coral Weddings*, and I hope you enjoyed these sweet family weddings. If you'd like to see what happens next in Summer Beach, join me for an old-fashioned centennial party in *Coral Celebration* for more heartwarming fun. When Marina volunteers to organize the beachside community's celebration, old rivalries and history surface.

If you've read the *Seabreeze Inn* at Summer Beach series, you're also invited to join the family reunion in Seabreeze Reunion, the next in that series.

And, discover a brand new branch of the family in *Beach View Lane*.

Keep up with my new releases on my website at JanMoran.com. Please join my VIP Reader's Club there to receive news about special deals and other goodies. Plus, find more fun and join other like-minded readers in my Facebook Reader's Group.

More to Enjoy

If this is your first book in the Coral Cottage series, be sure to meet Marina when she first arrives in Summer Beach in *Coral*

Cottage. If you haven't read the Seabreeze Inn at Summer Beach series, I invite you to meet art teacher Ivy Bay and her sister Shelly as they renovate a historic beach house in *Seabreeze Inn*, the first in the original Summer Beach series.

You might also enjoy more sunshine and international travel with a group of friends in the *Love California* series, beginning with *Flawless* and an exciting trip to Paris.

Finally, I invite you to read my standalone historical novels, including Hepburn's Necklace and The Chocolatier, a pair of 1950s sagas set in gorgeous Italy.

Most of my books are available in ebook, paperback or hardcover, audiobooks, and large print. And as always, I wish you happy reading!

CORAL WEDDINGS RECIPES

Sunshine Coolers
A Pineapple, Lime, and Ginger Delight

This is the refreshing cooler that Marina Moore mixed for her guests; it's also one I enjoy on a warm day by the beach. For the leanest version, use sugar-free ginger ale or sparkling water.

If I am making this for myself, I simply pour equal amounts of pineapple juice and ginger ale, then add the juice of lime and zest. Simple!

To convert your cooler into a light summer cocktail, add prosecco or champagne instead of ginger ale. If you prefer spirits such as tequila or rum, add after the pineapple mixture. Add 1 ounce (30 ml), and fill the remaining glass with ginger ale or soda.

Serves 4

1 Tbsp lime zest (15 grams)
2 Tbsp lime juice (1 ounce, 30 ml)
24 ounces pineapple juice (700 ml)

24 ounces ginger ale (or lemon-lime soda or sparkling water) (700 ml)
Garnish: sliced lime, fresh mint, sliced pineapple
Optional: Champagne, prosecco (to replace ginger ale); tequila or rum(1 ounce/30 ml)

Instructions

1. Combine lime zest and lime juice in a pitcher.
    2. Add pineapple juice and stir. Chill for 1 hour.
    3. In 4 glasses filled to 1/3 with ice, pour pineapple mixture to 2/3
    4. Fill remainder with ginger ale, soda, or sparkling water (or champagne or prosecco)
    5. Garnish with mint and lime slices.

Enjoy and drink responsibly.

Optional:
    For a sweeter taste profile, add simple syrup to the pitcher along with the pineapple and lime juice. Or add a few drops of stevia or monk fruit sweetener replacement.

Simple syrup:
    1. Combine 1/2 cup sugar (or honey) and 1/2 cup water in a saucepan.
    2. Heat on medium, stirring just until sugar dissolves.
    3. Cool to room temperature.

Avocado Gazpacho - Chilled Soup

This is Marina Moore's Coral Cafe recipe for a chilled summer soup. The addition of avocados creates a creamier version than the traditional Spanish gazpacho. In Southern California, avocados are plentiful, with different varieties ripening at various times, spring through fall. With local avocados, tomatoes, basil, lemon, and onions from my garden, this is a quick and easy meal that won't heat the kitchen. Look for the creamiest avocados, such as Hass or Reed varieties.

For added protein, you might include bay shrimp as an additional garnish. If you find the garlic and onion flavors too pungent, sauté lightly in olive oil before adding to the blender or food processor.

For a southwestern U.S.-inspired dish, garnish with cilantro, tortilla chips or strips, pepitas, and chunky salsa. Otherwise, basil and herb croutons are a nice garnish combination. If you know your guests' preferences, you may serve the finished gazpacho with garnishes. If not, serve garnishes in small bowls and let your guests add what they like.

Serves 4

3 medium-sized ripe avocados (or 2 large), 6 to 8 ounces (175 to 225grams)
1 1/2 pounds ripe tomatoes peeled and cored, or canned tomatoes (16 to 24 ounces), (450 to 650 grams)
2 to 5 cloves of garlic to taste
2 Tbsp yellow onions, diced (30 grams)
2 Tbsp yellow, and green peppers, diced (30 grams)
2 Tbsp extra virgin olive oil (60 ml)
Juice of 1 lemon or 1 Tbsp (30 ml)
1 Tbsp sherry vinegar or wine vinegar (30 ml)
1/2 to 1 cup (4 to 8 ounces) of chilled water (1/2 to 1 pint, 100 to 225 ml)
1/2 to 1 teaspoon sweet paprika (2 to 5 ml)
1/2 tsp kosher or sea salt, to taste (2 to 5 ml)
1/2 tsp cracked pepper, to taste (2 to 5 ml)

Optional Garnishes:

1/2 to 1 cup finely chopped tomato (100 to 225 ml)
1/2 to 1 cup finely chopped cucumber (100 to 225 ml)
1/2 to 1 cup finely chopped mango (100 to 225 ml)
3 Tbsp chopped fresh basil (50 grams)
3 Tbsp cilantro (50 grams)
1/2 cup tortilla chips or croutons (100 ml)
1 cup Bay (small) shrimp (225 ml)
Toasted pepitas, sprinkle

Instructions:

1. In a food processor or blender, combine chopped avocados, tomatoes, garlic, onion, pepper, olive oil, lemon juice, and sherry or wine vinegar. Puree until a smooth consistency is reached. Add seasonings to taste. Add chilled water a little at a time until desired consistency is reached. It should be velvety smooth, not too thick nor too thin. However, if you prefer your gazpacho a little chunky, reserve half the avocados and tomatoes to add at the end and pulse quickly.

2. Chill for 2 to 3 hours. Serve in large soup bowls with plenty of room for garnishes.

3. Serve soup cold with selected garnishes on top or on the side in small bowls.

4. Keeps in the refrigerator for 1 to 2 days. Note: Bright green avocado flesh naturally darkens when exposed to oxygen, although lemon juice helps maintain brightness. If your soup takes on a slightly brownish hue the next day, it is still good to eat. Stir well and serve.

ABOUT THE AUTHOR

JAN MORAN is a *USA Today* and a *Wall Street Journal* bestselling author of romantic women's fiction. A few of her favorite things include a fine cup of coffee, dark chocolate, fresh flowers, laughter, and music that touches her soul. She loves to travel, and her favorite places for inspiration are those rich with history and mystery and set against snowy mountains, palm-treed beaches, or sparkly city lights. Jan is originally from Austin, Texas, and a trace of a drawl still survives, although she has lived in Southern California near the beach for years.

Most of her books are available as audiobooks, and her historical fiction is translated into German, Italian, Polish, Dutch, Turkish, Russian, Bulgarian, Portuguese, and Lithuanian, and other languages.

If you enjoyed this book, please consider leaving a brief review online for your fellow readers where you purchased this book or on Goodreads or Bookbub.

To read Jan's other historical and contemporary novels, visit JanMoran.com. Join her VIP Readers Club mailing list and Facebook Readers Group to learn of new releases, sales and contests.

Made in the USA
Las Vegas, NV
24 July 2023

75161695R00135